A SLAV SOUL

A SLAV SOUL

AND OTHER STORIES

BY

ALEXANDER KUPRIN

WITH AN INTRODUCTION BY

STEPHEN GRAHAM

Short Story Index Reprint Series

BOOKS FOR LIBRARIES PRESS
FREEPORT, NEW YORK

First Published 1916
Reprinted 1971

INTERNATIONAL STANDARD BOOK NUMBER:
0-8369-3844-5

LIBRARY OF CONGRESS CATALOG CARD NUMBER:
78-150547

PRINTED IN THE UNITED STATES OF AMERICA

CONTENTS

INTRODUCTION

ALEXANDER KUPRIN

" Oh how incomprehensible for us, how mysterious, how strange are the very simplest happenings in life. And we, not understanding them, unable to penetrate their significance, heap one event upon another, plait them together, join them, make acquaintances and marriages, write books, say sermons, found ministries, carry on war or trade, make new inventions and then after all, create history ! And yet every time I think of the immensity and complexity, the incomprehensible and elemental accidentoriness of the whole hurly-burly of life, then my own little life seems but a miserable speck of dust lost in the whirl of a hurricane."

So in a paragraph in one of his sketches Alexander Kuprin gives his feelings about his life and his work, and in that expression perhaps we see his characteristic attitude towards the world of which he writes. One of the strongest tales in this collection, 'Tempting Providence," is very representative of Kuprin in this vein.

After Chekhof the most popular tale-writer in Russia is Kuprin, the author of fourteen volumes of effusive, touching and humorous stories. He is read by the great mass of the Russian reading public, and his works can be bought at any railway bookstall in the Empire. He is devoured by the students, loved by the bourgeois, and admired even by intellectual and fastidious Russians. It is impossible not to admire this natural torrent of Russian thoughts and words and sentiments. His lively pages are a reflection of Russia herself, and without having been once in the country it would be possible to get a fair notion of its surface life by reading these tales in translation. Perhaps the greatest of living Russian novelists is Kuprin—exalted, hysterical, sentimental, Rabelaisian Kuprin. He comes to you with a handful of wild flowers in one red, hairy hand and a shovelful of rubbish in the other—his shiny, lachrymose but unfathomable features pouring floods of tears or rolling and bursting in guffaws of laughter. His is a rank verbiage—he gives birth to words, ideas, examples in tens where other writers go by units and threes.

He is occasionally coarse, occasionally sentimental, but he gives great delight to his readers; his are rough-hewn lumps of conversation and life. With him everything is taken from life. He seems to be a master of detail, and the characteristic of his style is a tendency to give the most diverting lists. Often paragraph after paragraph, if you look into the style, would be found to be lists of delicious details reported in a conversational manner. Thus, opening a volume at random, you can easily find an example :—

"Imagine the village we had reached—all overblown with snow; the inevitable village idiot, Serozha, walking almost naked in the snow; the priest, who won't play cards the day before a festival but writes denunciations to the village starosta instead—a stupid, artful man, and an adept at getting alms, speaking an atrocious Petersburg Russian. If you have grasped what society was like in the village you know to what point of boredom and stupefaction we attained.

We had already got tired of bear-hunting, hare-hunting with hounds, pistol-shooting at a target through three rooms, writing humorous verses.   It must be confessed we quarrelled."

He is also the inventor of amusing sentences which can almost be used as proverbs :—

He knew which end of the asparagus to eat.

Or,

We looked at our neighbours through a microscope; they at us through a telescope.

Every one of Kuprin's stories has the necessary Attic salt. He is like our English Kipling, whom he greatly admires, and about whom he has written in one of his books an appreciative essay. He is also something like the American O. Henry, especially in the matter of his lists of details and his apt metaphors, but he has not the artifice nor the everlasting American smile. Kuprin, moreover, takes his matter from life and writes with great ease and carelessness ; O. Henry put together from life and re-wrote twelve times.

Above all things Kuprin is a sentimental author, preferring an impulse to a reason, and abandoning logic whenever his feelings are touched. He likes to feel the reader with the tears in his eyes and then to go forward with him in the unity of emotional friend-ship. There is, however, under this excitement a rather self-centred cynic despising the things he does not love, a satirical genius. His humour is nearly always at the expense of some person, institution or class of society. Thus " The Song and the Dance " is at the expense of the peasantry, " The Last Word " at the expense of the lower *intelligentia*, "The White Poodle " at the expense of those rich bourgeois who have villas on the Crimean shores, " Anathema " at the expense of the Church, " Mechanical Justice " at the expense of the professor, and so on. And it is part of Kuprin's sentiment to love dogs almost as much as men, and he tells no tales at dogs' expense. " The White Poodle " and " Dogs' Happiness " are two of his dog tales.

The tales selected are taken from various volumes, and two of them, " The Elephant " and " The White Poodle," from a volume specially designed by him for reading aloud to children. They are in very simple and colloquial and humorous Russian, and are delightful to read aloud.

Kuprin, who is a living Russian tale-writer, though considerably less productive than in his earlier years, spent a great deal of time in the Crimea, which is evidently favourite country to him. Chekhof also lived in the Crimea and tended lovingly his rose garden at Yalta. His neighbour, Kuprin, wrote one of the most charming reminiscent essays on Chekhof and his life in " To the Glory of the Living and the Dead," which also contains the Kipling essay. Many of Kuprin's stories relate to the Crimea, and the longest of these given in this selection contains a description of Crimean life, and gives (pp. 154—157) a wonderful impression of a Crimean summer night. Kuprin has also lived in England and has written tales of London life, and has occasional references to English characteristics. But I have avoided carrying coals to Newcastle.

As compared with Sologub, whose volume of beautiful tales, "The Sweet-scented Name," has found so many friends in England, Kuprin may be said to be nearer to the earth, less in the clouds.

He is a satirical realist, whereas Sologub is a fantastic realist. Sologub discloses the devils and the angels in men and women, but Kuprin is cheerfully human. Both have a certain satirical genius, but Kuprin is read by everyone, whereas it would be hardly one in ten that could follow Sologub. In comparison with Chekhof I should say Kuprin was a little more inventive, and as regards a picture of life Kuprin is nearer to the present moment. Nearly all these Russian tale-writers excel in describing the life of townspeople. Very little study of the peasantry has been made, though there are one or two notable exceptions.

Kuprin made his name in writing stories of life in the Russian army. He did not describe the common soldier as did his likeness, Kipling, but rather the life of the officers. His most famous books on the subject are "Cadets," "Staff-Captain Ribnikof"[1] and "The Duel."[1] He extended his popularity with somewhat lurid and oleographic descriptions of the night haunt and night life, and wrote the notorious novel, lately completed, entitled "*Yama*"—"The Pit." He has written a great deal about the relationship of men and women. His weakness is the subject of women. Whenever they come into question he becomes self-conscious and awkward, putting his subject in the wrong light, protesting too much, and finally writing that which is not fitting just because "all is permitted" and "why shouldn't we?" His poorest work is his coarse work. Nothing ugly is worth reproducing, however curious the ugliness may be. We do not want the ugly, and are interested more in brightest

[1] Now obtainable in English translation.

Russia than in darkest Russia. My purpose is to give what is beautiful, or in any case what is interesting but not ugly, in the living Russian literature of to-day. Consequently I have made, together with my wife, a choice of Kuprin. We have read all his stories through and taken fifteen of those which make him a great writer, just those which should enrich us. Here is Kuprin's humour, sentiment, pathos, and delightful and entertaining verbosity. Of this work all but three tales were translated by my wife, and these three by myself. I have communicated the contents to Kuprin, who sanctions the publication.

STEPHEN GRAHAM.

LONDON.

A SLAV SOUL

I

A SLAV SOUL

THE farther I go back in my memory of the past, and the nearer I get to remembering incidents connected with my childhood, the more confused and doubtful do my recollections become. Much, no doubt, was told me afterwards, in a more conscious stage of my existence, by those who, with loving care, noticed my early doings. Perhaps many of the things that I recall never happened to me ; I heard or read them some time or other and their remembrance grew to be part of myself. Who can guarantee which of these recollections are of real facts and which of tales told so long ago that they have all the appearance of truth—who can know where one ends and the other begins ?

My imagination recalls with special vividness the eccentric figure of Yasha and the two companions— I might almost call them friends—who accompanied him along the path of life : Matsko, an old rejected cavalry horse, and the yard-dog Bouton.

Yasha was distinguished by the deliberate slowness of his speech and actions, and he always had the air of a man whose thoughts were concentrated on himself. He spoke very seldom and considered his speech ; he tried to speak good Russian, though at times when he was moved he would burst out in his native dialect of Little-Russian. Owing to his dress of a dark colour and sober cut, and to the solemn and almost melancholy expression of his shaven face and thin pursed lips, he always gave the impression that he was an old servant of a noble family of the good old times.

Of all the human beings that he knew, Yasha seemed to find my father the only one besides himself worthy of his veneration. And though to us children, to my mother, and to all our family and friends, his manner was respectful, it was mingled with a certain pity and slighting condescension. It was always an enigma to me—whence came this immeasurable pride of his. Servants have often a well-known form of insolence ; they take upon themselves some of that attractive authority which they have noticed in their masters. But my father, a poor doctor in a little Jewish village, lived so modestly and quietly that Yasha could never have learnt from him to look down upon his neighbours. And in Yasha himself there was none of the ordinary insolence of a servant—he had no metropolitan polish and could not overawe people by using foreign words, he had no overbearing manners towards country chambermaids, no gentle art of tinkling out touching romances on the guitar, an art by which so many inexperienced souls have been ruined. He occupied his leisure hours in lying in sheer idleness full-length on the box in which he kept his belongings. He not only did not read books, but he sincerely despised them. All things written, except in the Bible, were, in his opinion, written not for truth's sake but just to get money, and he therefore preferred to any book those long rambling thoughts which he turned over in his mind as he lay idly on his bed.

Matsko, the horse, had been rejected from military service on account of many vices, the chief of which was that he was old, far too old. Then his forelegs were crooked, and at the places where they joined the body were adorned with bladder-like growths; he strutted on his hind legs like a cock. He held his head like a camel, and from old military habit tossed it upward and thrust his long neck forward. This, combined with his enormous size and unusual leanness, and the fact that he had only one eye, gave him a pitiful war-like and serio-comic expression. Such horses are called in the regiments " star-gazers."

Yasha prized Matsko much more than Bouton, who sometimes displayed a frivolity entirely out of keeping with his size. He was one of those shaggy, long-haired dogs who at times remind one of ferrets, but being ten times as large, they sometimes look like poodles ; they are by nature the very breed for yard-dogs. At home Bouton was always overwhelmingly serious and sensible in all his ways, but in the streets his behaviour was positively disgraceful. If he went out with my father he would never run modestly behind the carriage as a well-behaved dog should do. He would rush to meet all other dogs, jump about them and bark loudly in their very noses, only springing away to one side in affright if one of them with a snort of alarm bent his head quickly and tried to bite him. He ran into other people's yards and came tearing out again after a second or so, chased by a dozen angry dogs of the place. He wandered about on terms of deepest friend-ship with dogs of a known bad reputation,

In our districts of Podolia and Volhynia nothing was thought so much of as a person's way of setting out from his house. A squire might long since have mortgaged and re-mortgaged his estate, and be only waiting for the officers of the Crown to take possession of his property, but let him only on a Sunday go out to "Holy Church," it must be in a light tarantass drawn by four or six splendid fiery Polish horses, and driving into the market square of the village he must cry to the coachman—"Lay on with the whip, Joseph." Yet I am sure that none of our rich neighbours started off in such pomp as Yasha was able to impart to our equipage when my father made up his mind to journey forth. Yasha would put on a shining hat with a shade in front and behind, and a broad yellow belt. Then the carriage would be taken out about a hundred yards from the house—an antique coach of the old Polish days—and Matsko put in. Hardly would my father show himself at the house-door than Yasha would give a magnificent crack with his whip, Matsko would wave his tail some time in hesitation and then start at a sober trot, flinging out and raising his hind legs, and strutting like a cock. Coming level with the house-door Yasha would pretend that only with great difficulty could he restrain the impatient horses, stretching out both his arms and pulling back the reins with all his might. All his attention would seem to be swallowed up by the horses, and whatever might happen elsewhere round about him, Yasha would never turn his head. Probably he did all this to sustain our family honour.

Yasha had an extraordinarily high opinion of my father. It would happen upon occasion that some poor Jew or peasant would be waiting his turn in the anteroom while my father was occupied with another patient. Yasha would often enter into a conversation with him, with the simple object of increasing my father's popularity as a doctor.

" What do you think ? " he would ask, taking up a position of importance on a stool and surveying the patient before him from head to foot. " Perhaps you fancy that coming to my master is like asking medical advice of the clerk at the village police-station. My master not only stands higher than such a one, brother, but higher than the chief of police himself. He knows about everything in the world, my brother. Yes, he does. Now, what's the matter with you ? "

" There's something wrong with my inside . . .," the sick person would say, " my chest burns. . . ."

" Ah, you see—what causes that ? What will cure you ? You don't know, and I don't. But my master will only throw a glance at you and he'll tell you at once whether you'll live or die."

Yasha lived very economically, and he spent his money in buying various things which he carefully stored away in his large tin-bound wooden trunk. Nothing gave us children greater pleasure than for Yasha to let us look on while he turned out these things. On the inside of the lid of the trunk were pasted pictures of various kinds. There, side by side with portraits of terrifying green-whiskered generals who had fought for the fatherland, were pictures of martyrs, engravings from the *Neva*,[1] studies of women's heads, and fairy-tale pictures of the robber-

---

[1] A popular Russian magazine which presents its readers with many supplements.

swallow in an oak, opening wide his right eye to receive
the arrow of Ilya-Muromets.   Yasha would bring out
from the trunk a whole collection of coats, waistcoats,
top-coats, fur-caps, cups and saucers, wire boxes ornamented with false pearls and with transfer pictures
of flowers, and little circular mirrors.   Sometimes,
from a side pocket of the trunk, he would bring out an
apple or a couple of buns strewn with poppy-seed,
which we always found especially appetising.

Yasha was usually very precise and careful.   Once
he broke a large decanter and my father scolded him
for it.   The next day Yasha appeared with two new
decanters.   " I daresay I shall break another one," he
explained, " and anyhow we can find a use for the two
somehow."   He kept all the rooms of the house in
perfect cleanliness and order.   He was very jealous of
all his rights and duties, and he was firmly convinced
that no one could clean the floors as well as he.   At one
time he had a great quarrel with a new housemaid,
Yevka, as to which of them could clean out a room
better.   We were called in as expert judges, and in
order to tease Yasha a little we gave the palm to Yevka.
But children as we were, we didn't know the human
soul, and we little suspected what a cruel blow this was
to Yasha.   He went out of the room without saying a
word, and next day everybody in the village knew that
Yasha was drunk.

Yasha used to get drunk about two or three times a
year, and these were times of great unhappiness for him
and for all the family.   There was nobody then to chop
wood, to feed the horses, to bring in water.   For five or
six days we lost sight of Yasha and heard nothing of his
doings.   On the seventh day he came back without hat

or coat and in a dreadful condition. A crowd of noisy Jews followed about thirty paces behind him, and ragged urchins called names after him and made faces. They all knew that Yasha was going to hold an auction.

Yasha came into the house, and then in a minute or so ran out again into the street, carrying in his arms almost all the contents of his trunk. The crowd came round him quickly.

" How's that ? You won't give me any more vodka, won't you ? " he shouted, shaking out trousers and waistcoats and holding them up in his hands. " What, I haven't any more money, eh ? How much for this ? and this, and this ? "

And one after another he flung his garments among the crowd, who snatched at them with tens of rapacious fingers.

" How much'll you give ? " Yasha shouted to one of the Jews who had possessed himself of a coat—" how much'll you give, mare's head ? "

" We—ll, I'll give you fifty copecks," drawled the Jew, his eyes staring.

" Fifty copecks, fifty ? " Yasha seemed to fall into a frenzy of despair. " I don't want fifty copecks. Why not say twenty ? Give me gold ! What's this ? Towels ? Give me ten copecks for the lot, eh ? Oh that you had died of fever ! Oh that you had died when you were young ! "

Our village has its policeman, but his duties consist mainly in standing as godfather to the farmers' children, and on such an occasion as this " the police " took no share in quelling the disorder, but acted the part of a modest and silent looker-on. But my father, seeing the plunder of Yasha's property, could no longer restrain his rage and contempt. " He's got drunk again, the idiot, and now he'll lose all his goods," said he, unselfishly hurling himself into the crowd. In a second the people were gone and he found himself alone with Yasha, holding in his hands some pitiful-looking razor-case or other. Yasha staggered in astonishment, helplessly raising his eyebrows, and then he suddenly fell heavily on his knees.

" Master ! My own dear master ! See what they've done to me ! "

" Go off into the shed," ordered my father angrily, pulling himself away from Yasha, who had seized the tail of his coat and was kissing it. " Go into the shed and sleep off your drunkenness so that to-morrow even the smell of you may be gone ! "

Yasha went away humbly into the shed, and then began for him those tormenting hours of getting sober, the deep and oppressive torture of repentance. He lay on his stomach and rested his head on the palms of his hands, staring fixedly at some point in front of him. He knew perfectly well what was taking place in the house. He could picture to himself how we were all begging my father to forgive him, and how my father would impatiently wave his hands and refuse to listen. He knew very well that probably this time my father would be implacable.

Every now and then we children would be impelled by curiosity to go and listen at the door of the shed, and we would hear strange sounds as of bellowing and sobbing.

In such times of affliction and degradation Bouton counted it his moral duty to be in attendance upon the suffering Yasha. The sagacious creature knew very well that ordinarily when Yasha was sober he would never be allowed to show any sign of familiarity towards him. Whenever he met the stern figure of Yasha in the yard Bouton would put on an air of gazing attentively into the distance or of being entirely occupied in snapping at flies. We children used to fondle Bouton and feed him occasionally, we used to pull the burrs out of his shaggy coat while he stood in patient endurance, we even used to kiss him on his cold, wet nose. And I always wondered that Bouton's sympathy and devotion used to be given entirely to Yasha, from whom he seemed to get nothing but kicks. Now, alas! when bitter experience has taught me to look all round and on the under side of things, I begin to suspect that the source of Bouton's devotion was not really enigmatical—it was Yasha who fed Bouton every day, and brought him his dish of scraps after dinner.

In ordinary times, I say, Bouton would never have risked forcing himself upon Yasha's attention. But in these days of repentance he went daringly into the shed and planted himself by the side of Yasha, staring into a corner and breathing deeply and sympathetically. If this seemed to do no good, he would begin to lick his patron's face and hands, timidly at first, but afterwards boldly and more boldly. It would end by Yasha putting his arms round Bouton's neck and sobbing, then Bouton would insinuate himself by degrees under Yasha's body, and the voices of the two would mingle in a strange and touching duet.

Next day Yasha came into the house at early dawn, gloomy and downcast. He cleaned the floor and the furniture and put everything into a state of shining cleanliness ready for the coming of my father, the very thought of whom made Yasha tremble. But my father was not to be appeased. He handed Yasha his wages and his passport and ordered him to leave the place at once. Prayers and oaths of repentance were vain.

Then Yasha resolved to take extreme measures.

" So it means you're sending me away, sir, does it ? " he asked boldly.

" Yes, and at once."

" Well then, I won't go. You send me away now, and you'll simply all die off like beetles. I won't go. I'll stay years ! "

" I shall send for the policeman to take you off."

" Take me off," said Yasha in amazement. " Well, let him. All the town knows that I've served you faithfully for twenty years, and then I'm sent off by the police. Let them take me. It won't be shame to me but to you, sir ! "

And Yasha really stayed on. Threats had no effect upon him. He paid no attention to them, but worked untiringly in an exaggerated way, trying to make up for lost time. That night he didn't go into the kitchen to sleep, but lay down in Matsko's stall, and the horse stood up all night, afraid to move and unable to lie down in his accustomed place. My father was a good-natured and indolent man, who easily submitted himself to surrounding circumstances and to people and things with which he was familiar. By the evening he had forgiven Yasha.

Yasha was a handsome man, of a fair, Little-Russian, melancholy type. Young men and girls looked admiringly at him, but not one of them running like a quail across the yard would have dared to give him a playful punch in the side or even an inviting smile—

there was too much haughtiness in him and icy contempt for the fair sex. And the delights of a family hearth seemed to have little attraction for him. "When a woman establishes herself in a cottage," he used to say intolerantly, "the air becomes bad at once." However, he did once make a move in that direction, and then he surprised us more than ever before. We were seated at tea one evening when Yasha came into the dining-room. He was perfectly sober, but his face wore a look of agitation, and pointing mysteriously with his thumb over his shoulder towards the door, he asked in a whisper, "Can I bring them in?"

"Who is it?" asked father. "Let them come in."

All eyes were turned in expectation towards the door, from behind which there crept a strange being. It was a woman of over fifty years of age, ragged, drunken, degraded and foolish-looking.

"Give us your blessing, sir, we're going to be married," said Yasha, dropping on his knees. "Get down on your knees, fool," cried he, addressing the woman and pulling her roughly by the sleeve.

My father with difficulty overcame his astonishment. He talked to Yasha long and earnestly, and told him he must be going out of his mind to think of marrying such a creature. Yasha listened in silence, not getting up from his knees; the silly woman knelt too all the time.

"So you don't allow us to marry, sir?" asked Yasha at last.

"Not only do I not allow you, but I'm quite sure you won't do such a thing," answered my father.

"That means that I won't," said Yasha resolutely. "Get up, you fool," said he, turning to the woman. "You hear what the master says. Go away at once."

And with these words he hauled the unexpected guest away by the collar, and they both went quickly out of the room.

This was the only attempt Yasha made towards the state of matrimony. Each of us explained the affair to ourselves in our own way, but we never understood it fully, for whenever we asked Yasha further about it, he only waved his hands in vexation.

Still more mysterious and unexpected was his death. It happened so suddenly and enigmatically and had apparently so little connection with any previous circumstance in Yasha's life that if I were forced to recount what happened I feel I couldn't do it at all well. Yet all the same, I am confident that what I say really took place, and that none of the clear impression of it is at all exaggerated.

One day, in the railway station three versts from the village, a certain well-dressed young man, a passenger from one of the trains, hanged himself in a lavatory. Yasha at once asked my father if he might go and see the body.

Four hours later he returned and went straight into the dining-room—we had visitors at the time—and stood by the door. It was only two days after one of his drinking bouts and repentance in the shed, and he was quite sober.

" What is it ? " asked my mother.

Yasha suddenly burst into a guffaw. " He—he—he," said he. " His tongue was all hanging out. . . . The gentleman. . . ."

My father ordered him into the kitchen. Our guests talked a little about Yasha's idiosyncrasies and then soon forgot about the little incident. Next day, about eight o'clock in the evening, Yasha went up to my little sister in the nursery and kissed her.

" Good-bye, missy."

" Good-bye, Yasha," answered the little one, not looking up from her doll.

Half an hour later Yevka, the housemaid, ran into my father's study, pale and trembling.

" Oh, sir . . . there . . . in the attic . . . he's hanged himself . . . Yasha. . . ."

And she fell down in a swoon.

On a nail in the attic hung the lifeless body of Yasha. When the coroner questioned the cook, she said that Yasha's manner had been very strange on the day of his death.

" He stood before the looking-glass," said she, " and pressed his hands so tightly round his neck that his face went quite red and his tongue stuck out and his eyes bulged. . . . He must have been seeing what he would look like."

The coroner brought in a verdict of " suicide while in a state of unsound mind."

Yasha was buried in a special grave dug for the purpose in the ravine on the other side of the wood. Next day Bouton could not be found anywhere. The faithful dog had run off to the grave and lay there howling, mourning the death of his austere friend. Afterwards he disappeared and we never saw him again.

And now that I myself am nearly what may be called an old man, I go over my varied recollections now and then, and when I come to the thought of Yasha, every time I say to myself: " What a strange soul—faithful, pure, contradictory, absurd—and great. Was it not a truly Slav soul that dwelt in the body of Yasha ? "

THE SONG AND THE DANCE

WE lived at that time in the Government of Riazan, some 120 versts from the nearest railway station and even 25 versts from the large trading village of Tuma. " Tuma is iron and its people are of stone," as the local inhabitants say of themselves. We lived on an old untenanted estate, where in 1812 an immense house of wood had been constructed to accommodate the French prisoners. The house had columns, and a park with lime trees had been made around it to remind the prisoners of Versailles.

Imagine our comical situation. There were twenty-three rooms at our disposal, but only one of them had a stove and was warmed, and even in that room it was so cold that water froze in it in the early morning and the door was frosted at the fastenings. The post came sometimes once a week, sometimes once in two months, and was brought by a chance peasant, generally an old man with the packet under his shaggy snow-strewn coat, the addresses wet and smudged, the backs unsealed and stuck again by inquisitive postmasters. Around us was an ancient pine wood where bears prowled, and whence even in broad daylight the hungry wolves sallied forth and snatched away yawning dogs from the street of the hamlet near by. The local population spoke in a dialect we did not understand, now in a sing-song drawl, now coughing and hooting, and they stared at us surlily and without restraint. They were firmly convinced that the forest belonged to God and the muzhik alone, and the lazy German steward only knew how much wood they stole. There was at our service a splendid French library of the eighteenth century, though all the magnificent bindings were mouse-eaten. There was an old portrait gallery with the canvases ruined from damp, mould, and smoke.

Picture to yourself the neighbouring hamlet all overblown with snow, and the inevitable village idiot, Serozha, who goes naked even in the coldest weather ; the priest who does not play " preference " on a fast day, but writes denunciations to the starosta, a stupid, artful man, diplomat and beggar, speaking in a dreadful Petersburg accent. If you see all this you understand to what a degree of boredom we attained. We grew tired of encompassing bears, of hunting hares with hounds, of shooting with pistols at a target through three rooms at a distance of twenty-five paces, of writing humorous verses in the evening. Of course we quarrelled.

Yes, and if you had asked us individually why we had come to this place I should think not one of us would have answered the question. I was painting at that time ; Valerian Alexandrovitch wrote symbolical verses, and Vaska amused himself with Wagner and played Tristan and Iseult on the old, ruined, yellow-keyed clavicordia.

But about Chirstmas-time the village began to enliven, and in all the little clearings round about, in Tristenka, in Borodina, Breslina, Shustova, Nikiforskaya and Kosli the peasants began to brew beer—such thick beer that it stained your hands and face at the touch, like lime bark. There was so much drunkenness among the peasants, even before the festival, that in Dagileva a son broke his father's head, and in Kruglitsi an old man drank himself to death. But Christmas was a diversion for us. We started paying the customary visits and offering congratulations to all the local officials and peasants of our acquaintance. First we went to the priest, then to the psalm-singer of the church, then to the church watchman, then to the two school-mistresses. After the school-mistresses we fared more pleasantly. We turned up at the doctor's at Tuma, then trooped off to the district clerk, where a real banquet awaited us, then to the policeman, then to the lame apothecary, then to the local peasant tyrant who had grown rich and held a score of other peasants in his own grasp, and possessed all the cord, linen, grain, wood, whips in the neighbourhood. And we went and went on !

It must be confessed, however, that we felt a little awkward now and then. We couldn't manage to get into the *tempo* of the life there. We were really out of it. This life had creamed and mantled for years without number. In spite of our pleasant manners and apparent ease we were, all the same, people from another planet. Then there was a disparity in our mutual estimation of one another : we looked at them as through a microscope, they at us as through a telescope. Certainly we made attempts to accommodate ourselves, and when the psalm-singer's servant, a woman of forty, with warty hands all chocolate colour from the reins of the horse she put in the sledge when she went with a bucket to the well, sang of an evening, we did what we thought we ought to do. She would look ashamed, lower her eyes, fold her arms and sing:

> "Andray Nikolaevitch
> We have come to you,
> We wish to trouble you.
> But we have come
> And please to take
> The one of us you love."

Then we would boldly make to kiss her on the lips, which we did in spite of feigned resistance and screams.

And we would make a circle. One day there were a lot of us there; four students on holiday from an ecclesiastical college, the psalm-singer, a housekeeper from a neighbouring estate, the two school-mistresses, the policeman in his uniform, the deacon, the local horse-doctor, and we three æsthetes. We went round and round in a dance, and sang, roared, swinging now this way, now that, and the lion of the company, a student named Vozdvizhensky, stood in the middle and ordered our movements, dancing himself the while and snapping his fingers over his head:

> "The queen was in the town, yes, the town,
> And the prince, the little prince, ran away.
> Found a bride, did the prince, found a bride.
> She was nice, yes she was, she was nice,
> And a ring got the prince for her, a ring."

After a while the giddy whirl of the dance came to an end, and we stopped and began to sing to one another, in solemn tones:

> "The royal gates were opened,
> Bowed the king to the queen,
> And the queen to the king,
> But lower bowed the queen."

And then the horse-doctor and the psalm-singer had a competition as to who should bow lower to the other.

* * * * *

Our visiting continued, and at last came to the school-house at Tuma. That was inevitable, since there had been long rehearsals of an entertainment which the children were going to give entirely for our benefit—Petersburg guests. We went in. The Christmas tree was lit simultaneously by a touch-paper. As for the programme, I knew it by heart before we went in. There were several little tableaux, illustrative of songs of the countryside. It was all poorly done, but it must be confessed that one six-year-old mite playing the part of a peasant, wearing a huge cap of dog-skin and his father's great leather gloves with only places for hand and thumb, was delightful, with his serious face and hoarse little bass voice—a born artist.

The remainder was very disgusting. All done in the false popular style.

I had long been familiar with the usual entertainment items : Little-Russian songs mispronounced to an impossible point ; verses and silly embroidery patterns: " There's a Christmas tree, there's Petrushka, there's a horse, there's a steam-engine." The teacher, a little consumptive fellow, got up for the occasion in a long frock-coat and stiff shirt, played the fiddle in fits and starts, or beat time with his bow, or tapped a child on the head with it now and then.

The honorary guardian of the school, a notary from another town, chewed his gums all the time and stuck out his short parrot's tongue with sheer delight, feeling that the whole show had been got up in his honour.

At last the teacher got to the most important item

on his programme. We had laughed up till then, our turn was coming to weep. A little girl of twelve or thirteen came out, the daughter of a watchman, her face, by the way, not at all like his horse-like profile. She was the top girl in the school and she began her little song:

> " The jumping little grasshopper sang the summer through,
> Never once considering how the winter would blow in
> his eyes."

Then a shaggy little boy of seven, in his father's felt boots, took up his part, addressing the watchman's daughter:

> " That's strange, neighbour. Didn't you work in the
> summer ? "
> " What was there to work for ? There was plenty of
> grass."

Where was our famous Russian hospitality ?

To the question, " What did you do in the summer ? " the grasshopper could only reply, " I sang all the time."

At this answer the teacher, Kapitonitch, waved his bow and his fiddle at one and the same time—oh, that was an effect rehearsed long before that evening !— and suddenly in a mysterious half-whisper the whole choir began to sing:

> " You've sung your song, you call that doing,
> You've sung all the summer, then dance all the winter,
> You've sung your song, then dance all the winter,
> Dance all the winter, dance all the winter,
> You've sung the song, then dance the dance."

I confess that my hair stood on end as if each individual hair were made of glass, and it seemed to me as if the eyes of the children and of the peasants packing the schoolroom were all fixed on me as if repeating that d——d phrase :

"You've sung the song, you call that doing,
You've sung the song, then dance the dance."

I don't know how long this drone of evil boding and sinister recitation went on. But I remember clearly that during those minutes an appalling idea went through my brain. " Here we stand," thought I, " a little band of *intelligentsia*, face to face with an innumerable peasantry, the most enigmatical, the greatest, and the most abased people in the world. What connects us with them ? Nothing. Neither language, nor religion, nor labour, nor art. Our poetry would be ridiculous to their ears, absurd, incomprehensible. Our refined painting would be simply useless and senseless smudging in their eyes. Our quest for gods and making of gods would seem to them stupidity, our music merely a tedious noise. Our science would not satisfy them. Our complex work would seem laughable or pitiful to them, the austere and patient labourers of the fields. Yes. On the dreadful day of reckoning what answer shall we give to this child, wild beast, wise man, and animal, to this many-million-headed giant ? " We shall only be able to say sorrowfully, " We sang all the time. We sang our song."

And he will reply with an artful peasant smile, " Then go and dance the dance."

And I know that my companions felt as I did. We went out of the entertainment-room silent, not exchanging opinions.

Three days later we said good-bye, and since that time have been rather cold towards one another. We had been suddenly chilled in our consciences and made ashamed, as if these innocent mouths of sleepy children had pronounced death sentence upon us. And when I returned from the post of Ivan Karaulof to Goreli, and from Goreli to Koslof, and from Koslof to Zintabrof, and then further by railroad there followed me all the time that ironical, seemingly malicious phrase, " Then dance the dance."

God alone knows the destiny of the Russian people. . . . Well, I suppose, if it should be necessary, we'll dance it !

I travelled a whole night to the railway station.

On the bare frosted branches of the birches sat the stars, as if the Lord Himself had with His own hands decorated the trees. And I thought, " Yes, it's beautiful." But I could not banish that ironical thought, " Then dance the dance."

III

EASTER DAY

On his way from Petersburg to the Crimea Colonel Voznitsin purposely broke his journey at Moscow, where his childhood and youth had been spent, and stayed there two days. It is said that some animals when they feel that they are about to die go round to all their favourite and familiar haunts, taking leave of them, as it were. Voznitsin was not threatened by the near approach of death; at forty years of age he was still strong and well-preserved. But in his tastes and feelings and in his relations with the world he had reached the point from which life slips almost imperceptibly into old age. He had begun to narrow the circle of his enjoyments and pleasures; a habit of retrospection and of sceptical suspicion was manifest in his behaviour; his dumb, unconscious, animal love of Nature had become less and was giving place to a more refined appreciation of the shades of beauty; he was no longer agitated and disturbed by the adorable loveliness of women, but chiefly—and this was the first sign of spiritual blight—he began to think about his own death. Formerly he had thought about it in a careless and transient fashion—sooner or later death would come, not to him personally, but to some other, someone of the name of Voznitsin. But now he thought of it with a grievous, sharp, cruel, unwavering, merciless clearness, so that at nights his heart beat in terror and his blood ran cold. It was this feeling which had impelled him to visit once more those places familiar to his youth, to live over again in memory those dear, painfully sweet recollections of his childhood, overshadowed with a poetical sadness, to wound his soul once more with the sweet grief of recalling that which was for ever past—the irrevocable purity and clearness of his first impressions of life.

And so he did. He stayed two days in Moscow, returning to his old haunts. He went to see the boarding-house where once he had lived for six years in the charge of his form mistress, being educated under the Froebelian system. Everything there was altered and reconstituted ; the boys' department no longer existed, but in the girls' class-rooms there was still the pleasant and alluring smell of freshly varnished tables and stools ; there was still the marvellous mixture of odours in the dining-room, with a special smell of the apples which now, as then, the scholars hid in their private cupboards. He visited his old military school, and went into the private chapel where as a cadet he used to serve at the altar, swinging the censer and coming out in his surplice with a candle at the reading of the Gospel, but also stealing the wax candle-ends, drinking the wine after Communion, and sometimes making grimaces at the funny deacon and sending him into fits of laughter, so that once he was solemnly sent away from the altar by the priest, a magnificent and plump greybeard, strikingly like the picture of the God of Sabaoth behind the altar. He went along all the old streets, and purposely lingered in front of the houses where first of all had come to him the naïve and childish languishments of love ; he went into the courtyards and up the staircases, hardly recognising any of them, so much alteration and rebuilding had taken place in the quarter of a century of his absence. And he noticed with irritation and surprise that his staled and life-wearied soul remained cold and unmoved, and did not reflect in itself the old familiar grief for the past, that gentle grief, so bright, so calm, reflective and submissive.

" Yes, yes, yes—it's old age," he repeated to himself, nodding his head sadly. . . . " Old age, old age, old age. . . . It can't be helped. . . ."

After he left Moscow he was kept in Kief for a whole day on business, and only arrived at Odessa at the beginning of Holy Week. But it had been bad weather for some days, and Voznitsin, who was a very bad sailor, could not make up his mind to embark. It was only on the morning of Easter Eve that the weather became fine and the sea calm.

At six o'clock in the evening the steamer *Grand Duke Alexis* left the harbour. Voznitsin had no one to see him off, for which he was thankful. He had no patience with the somewhat hypocritical and always difficult comedy of farewell, when God knows why one stands a full half-hour at the side of the boat and looks down upon the people standing on the pier, smiling constrained smiles, throwing kisses, calling out from time to time in a theatrical tone foolish and meaningless phrases for the benefit of the bystanders, till at last, with a sigh of relief, one feels the steamer begin slowly and heavily to move away.

There were very few passengers on board, and the

majority of them were third-class people. In the first-class there were only two others besides himself a lady and her daughter, as the steward informed him. " That's good," thought he to himself.

Everything promised a smooth and easy voyage. His cabin was excellent, large and well lighted, with two divans and no upper berths at all. The sea, though gently tossing, grew gradually calmer, and the ship did not roll. At sunset, however, there was a fresh breeze on deck.

Voznitsin slept that night with open windows, and more soundly than he had slept for many months, perhaps for a year past. When the boat arrived at Eupatoria he was awakened by the noise of the cranes and by the running of the sailors on the deck. He got up, dressed quickly, ordered a glass of tea, and went above.

The steamer was at anchor in a half-transparent mist of a milky rose tint, pierced by the golden rays of the rising sun. Scarcely noticeable in the distance, the flat shore lay glimmering. The sea was gently lapping the steamer's sides. There was a marvellous odour of fish, pitch and seaweed. From a barge alongside they were lading packages and bales. The captain's directions rang out clearly in the pure air of morning : " Maina, véra, véra po malu, stop ! "

When the barge had gone off and the steamer began to move again, Voznitsin went down into the dining saloon. A strange sight met his gaze. The tables were placed flat against the walls of the long room and were decorated with gay flowers and covered with Easter fare. There were lambs roasted whole, and turkeys, with their long necks supported by unseen rods and wire, raised their foolish heads on high. Their thin necks were bent into the form of an interrogation mark, and they trembled and shook with every movement of the steamer. They might have been strange antediluvian beasts, like the brontozauri or ichthauri one sees in pictures, lying there upon the large dishes, their legs bent under them, their heads on their twisted necks looking around with a comical and cautious wariness. The clear sunlight streamed through the port-holes and made golden circles of light on the tablecloths, transforming the colours of the Easter eggs into purple and sapphire, and making the flowers—hyacinths, pansies, tulips, violets, wallflowers, forget-me-nots—glow with living fire.

The other first-class passenger also came down for tea. Voznitsin threw a passing glance at her. She was neither young nor beautiful, but she had a tall, well-preserved, rather stout figure, and was well and simply dressed in an ample light-coloured cloak with silk collar and cuffs. Her head was covered with a light-blue, semi-transparent gauze scarf. She drank her tea and read a book at the same time, a French book Voznitsin judged by its small compact shape and pale yellow cover.

There was something strangely and remotely familiar about her, not so much in her face as in the turn of her neck and the lift of her eyebrows when she cast an answering glance at him. But this unconscious impression was soon dispersed and forgotten.

The heat of the saloon soon sent the passengers on deck, and they sat down on the seats on the sheltered side of the boat. The lady continued to read, though she often let her book fall on to her knee while she gazed upon the sea, on the dolphins sporting there, on the distant cliffs of the shore, purple in colour or covered with a scant verdure.

Voznitsin began to pace up and down the deck, turning when he reached the cabin. Once, as he passed the lady, she looked up at him attentively with a kind of questioning curiosity, and once more it seemed to him that he had met her before somewhere. Little by little this insistent feeling began to disquiet him, and he felt that the lady was experiencing the same feelings. But try as he would he could not remember meeting her before.

Suddenly, passing her for the twentieth time, he almost involuntarily stopped in front of her, saluted in military fashion, and lightly clicking his spurs together said:

" Pardon my boldness . . . but I can't get rid of a feeling that I know you, or rather that long ago I used to know you."

She was quite a plain woman, of blonde almost red colouring, grey hair—though this was only noticeable at a near view owing to its original light colour— pale eyelashes over blue eyes, and a faded freckled face. Her mouth only seemed fresh, being full and rosy, with beautifully curved lips.

" And I also," said she. " Just fancy, I've been sitting here and wondering where we could have met. My name is Lvova—does that remind you of anything ? "

" I'm sorry to say it doesn't," answered he, " but my name is Voznitsin."

The lady's eyes gleamed suddenly with a gay and

familiar smile, and Voznitsin saw that she knew him
at once.

" Voznitsin, Kolya Voznitsin," she cried joyfully,
holding out her hand to him. " Is it possible I didn't
recognise you ? Lvova, of course, is my married
name. . . . But no, no, you will remember me in
time. . . . Think : Moscow, Borisoglebsky Street,
the house belonging to the church. . . . Well ? Don't
you remember your school chum, Arkasha Yurlof . . . ? "

Voznitsin's hand trembled as he pressed hers.
A flash of memory enlightened him.

" Well, I never ! . . . It can't be Lenotchka ?
I beg your pardon, Elena . . . Elena. . . ."

" Elena Vladimirovna," she put in. " You've forgotten. . . . But you, Kolya, you're just the same
Kolya, awkward, shy, touchy Kolya. How strange
for us to meet like this ! Do sit down. . . . How
glad I am. . . ."

" Yes," muttered Voznitsin, " the world is really
so small that everyone must of necessity meet everyone
else "—a by no means original thought. " But tell
me all that has happened. How is Arkasha—and
Alexandra Millievna—and Oletchka ? "

At school Voznitsin had only been intimate with
one of his companions—Arkasha Yurlof. Every
Sunday he had leave he used to visit the family,
and at Easter and Christmas-time he had sometimes
spent his holidays with them. Before the time came
for them to go to college, Arkasha had fallen ill and
had been ordered away into the country. And from
that time Voznitsin had lost sight of him. Many
years ago he had heard by chance that Lenotchka
had been betrothed to an officer having the unusual

surname of Jenishek, who had done a thing at once
foolish and unexpected—shot himself.

"Arkasha died at our country house in 1890,"
answered the lady, "of cancer. And mother only
lived a year after. Oletchka took her medical degree
and is now a doctor in the Serdobsky district—before
that she was assistant in our village of Jemakino.
She has never wished to marry, though she's had many
good offers. I've been married twenty years," said
she, a gleam of a smile on her compressed lips. "I'm
quite an old woman. . . . My husband has an estate
in the country, and is a member of the Provincial
Council. He hasn't received many honours, but
he's an honest fellow and a good husband, is not a
drunkard, neither plays cards nor runs after women,
as others do. . . . God be praised for that ! . . ."

"Do you remember, Elena Vladimirovna, how I
was in love with you at one time ? " Voznitsin broke
in suddenly.

She smiled, and her face at once wore a look of
youth. Voznitsin saw for a moment the gleam of the
gold stopping in her teeth.

"Foolishness ! . . . Just lad's love. . . . But you
weren't in love with me at all ; you fell in love with
the Sinyelnikofs, all four of them, one after the other.
When the eldest girl married you placed your heart
at the feet of the next sister, and so on."

"Ah-ha ! You were just a little jealous, eh ? "
remarked Voznitsin with jocular self-satisfaction.

"Oh, not at all ! . . . You were like Arkasha's
brother. . . . Afterwards, later, when you were about
seventeen perhaps, I was a little vexed to think you
had changed towards me. . . . You know, its ridicu-

lous, but girls have hearts like women. We may not
love a silent adorer, but we are jealous if he pays
attentions to others. . . . But that's all nonsense.
Tell me more about yourself, where you live, and what
you do."

He told her of his life—at college, in the army,
about the war, and his present position. No, he had
never married—at first he had feared poverty and the
responsibility of a family, and now it was too late.
He had had flirtations, of course, and even some
serious romances.

The conversation ceased after a while, and they
sat silent, looking at one another with tender, tear-
dimmed eyes. In Voznitsin's memory the long past
of thirty years ago came swiftly again before him.
He had known Lenotchka when he was eleven years
old. She had been a naughty, fidgetty sort of girl,
fond of telling tales and liking to make trouble. Her
face was covered with freckles, she had long arms
and legs, pale eyelashes, and disorderly red hair
hanging about her face in long wisps. Her sister
Oletchka was different ; she had always kept apart,
and behaved like a sensible girl. On holidays they
all went together to dances at the Assembly Rooms,
to the theatre, the circus, to the skating rink. They
got up Christmas parties and children's plays together ;
they coloured eggs at Easter and dressed up at Christmas. They quarrelled and carried on together like
young puppies.

There were three years of that. Lenotchka used
to go away every summer with her people to their
country house at Jemakino, and that year, when she
returned to Moscow in the autumn, Voznitsin opened

both eyes and mouth in astonishment. She was changed ; you couldn't say that she was beautiful, but there was something in her face more wonderful than actual beauty, a rosy radiant blossoming of the feminine being in 'her. It is so sometimes. God knows how the miracle takes place, but in a few weeks, an awkward, undersized, gawky schoolgirl will develop suddenly into a charming maiden. Lenotchka's face still kept her summer sunburn, under which her ardent young blood flowed gaily, her shoulders had filled out, her figure rounded itself, and her soft breasts had a firm outline—all her body had become willowy, graceful, gracious.

And their relations towards one another had changed also. They became different after' one Saturday evening when the two of them, frolicking together before church service in a dimly lighted room, began to wrestle together and fight. The windows were wide open, and from the garden came the clear freshness of autumn and a slight winey odour of fallen leaves, and slowly one after another rang out the sounds of the church bells.

They struggled together ; their arms were round each other so that their bodies were pressed closely together and they were breathing in each other's faces. Suddenly Lenotchka, her face flaming crimson even in the darkening twilight, her eyes dilated, began to whisper angrily and confusedly :

" Let me go . . . let go. . . . I don't want to . . .," adding with a malicious gleam in her wet eyes : " Nasty, horrid boy."

The nasty, horrid boy released her and stood there, awkwardly stretching out his trembling arms. His

legs trembled also, and his forehead was wet with a
sudden perspiration. He had just now felt in his
arms the slender responsive waist of a woman, broaden-
ing out so wonderfully to the rounded hips ; he had
felt on his bosom the pliant yielding contact of her
firm, high, girlish breasts and breathed the perfume of
her body—that pleasant intoxicating scent of opening
poplar buds and young shoots of black-currant bushes
which one smells on a clear damp evening of spring
after a slight shower, when the sky and the rain-pools
flame with crimson and the may beetles hum in the air.

Thus began for Voznitsin that year of love languish-
ment, of bitter passionate dreams, of secret and
solitary tears. He became wild, unsociable, rude
and awkward in consequence of his torturing shyness ;
he was always knocking over chairs and catching
his clothes on the furniture, upsetting the tea-table
with all the cups and saucers—— "Our Kolinka's
always getting into trouble," said Lenotchka's mother
good-naturedly.

Lenotchka laughed at him. But he knew nothing
of it, he was continually behind her watching her
draw or write or embroider, and looking at the curve
of her neck with a strange mixture of happiness and
torture, watching her white skin and flowing golden
hair, seeing how her brown school-blouse moved with
her breathing, becoming large and wrinkling up into
little pleats when she drew in her breath, then filling
out and becoming tight and elastic and round again.
The sight of her girlish wrists and pretty arms, and
the scent of opening poplar buds about her, remained
with the boy and occupied his thoughts in class, in
church, in detention rooms.

In all his notebooks and textbooks Voznitsin drew beautifully-twined initials E and Y, and cut them with a knife on the lid of his desk in the middle of a pierced and flaming heart. The girl, with her woman's instinct, no doubt guessed his silent adoration, but in her eyes he was too everyday, too much one of the family. For him she had suddenly been transformed into a blooming, dazzling, fragrant wonder, but in her sight he was still the same impetuous boy as before, with a deep voice and hard rough hands, wearing a tight uniform and wide trousers. She coquetted innocently with her schoolboy friends and with the young son of the priest at the church, and, like a kitten sharpening its claws, she sometimes found it amusing to throw on Voznitsin a swift, burning, cunning glance. But if he in a momentary forgetfulness squeezed her hand too tightly, she would threaten him with a rosy finger and say meaningly :

" Take care, Kolya. I shall tell mother." And Voznitsin would shiver with unfeigned terror.

It was no wonder that Kolya had to spend two years in the sixth form ; no wonder either that in the summer he fell in love with the eldest of the Sinyelnikof girls, with whom he had once danced at a party. . . . But at Easter his full heart of love knew a moment of heavenly blessedness.

On Easter Eve he went with the Yurlofs to Borisoglebsky Church, where Alexandra Millievna had an honoured place, with her own kneeling-mat and soft folding chair. And somehow or other he contrived to come home alone with Lenotchka. The mother and Oletchka stayed for the consecration of the Easter cakes, and Lenotchka, Arkasha and Kolya came out of church together. But Arkasha diplomatically vanished—he disappeared as suddenly as if the earth had opened and swallowed him up. The two young people found themselves alone.

They went arm in arm through the crowd, their young legs moving easily and swiftly. Both were overcome by the beauty of the night, the joyous hymns, the multitude of lights, the Easter kisses, the smiles and greetings in the church. Outside there was a cheerful crowd of people ; the dark and tender sky was full of brightly twinkling stars ; the scent of moist young leaves was wafted from gardens, and they, too, were unexpectedly so near to one another they seemed lost together in the crowd, and they were out at an unusually late hour.

Pretending to himself that it was by accident, Voznitsin pressed Lenotchka's elbow to his side, and she answered with a barely noticeable movement in return. He repeated the secret caress, and she again responded. Then in the darkness he felt for her finger-tips and gently stroked them, and her hand made no objection, was not snatched away.

And so they came to the gate of the church house. Arkasha had left the little gate open for them. Narrow wooden planks placed over the mud led up to the house between two rows of spreading old lime trees. When the gate closed after them, Voznitsin caught Lenotchka's hand and began to kiss her fingers, so warm, so soft, so full of life.

" Lenotchka, I love you ; I love you. . . ."

He put his arms around her and kissed her in the darkness, somewhere just below her ear. His hat fell off on to the ground, but he did not stop to pick it up. He kissed the girl's cool cheek, and whispered as in a dream :

" Lenotchka, I love you, I love you. . . ."

" No, no," said she in a whisper, and hearing the whisper he sought her lips. " No, no, let me go; let me . . ."

Dear lips of hers, half childish, simple, innocent lips. When he kissed her she made no opposition, yet she did not return his kisses ; she breathed in a touching manner, quickly, deeply, submissively. Down his cheeks there flowed cool tears, tears of rapture. And when he drew his lips away from hers and looked up into the sky, the stars shining through the lime branches seemed to dance and come towards one another, to meet and swim together in silvery clusters, seen through his flowing tears.

" Lenotchka, I love you. . . ."

" Let me go. . . ."

" Lenotchka ! "

But suddenly she cried out angrily : " Let me go, you nasty, horrid boy. You'll see, I'll tell mother everything ; I'll tell her all about it. Indeed, I will."

She didn't say anything to her mother, but after that night she never allowed Voznitsin to be alone with her. And then the summer-time came. . . .

*   *   *   *   *

" And do you remember, Elena Vladimirovna, how one beautiful Easter night two young people kissed one another just inside the church-house gate ? " asked Voznitsin.

"No, I don't remember anything. . . . Nasty, horrid

boy," said the lady, smiling gently. "But look, here comes my daughter. You must make her acquaintance."

"Lenotchka, this is Nikolai Ivanitch Voznitsin, my old, old friend. I knew him as a child. And this is my Lenotchka. She's just exactly the same age as I was on that Easter night. . . ."

"Big Lenotchka and little Lenotchka," said Voznitsin.

"No, old Lenotchka and young Lenotchka," she answered, simply and quietly.

Lenotchka was very much like her mother, but taller and more beautiful than she had been in her youth. Her hair was not red, but the colour of a hazel nut with a brilliant lustre ; her dark eyebrows were finely and clearly outlined ; her mouth full and sensitive, fresh and beautiful.

The young girl was interested in the floating light-ships, and Voznitsin explained their construction and use. Then they talked about stationary lighthouses, the depth of the Black Sea, about divers, about collisions of steamers, and so on. Voznitsin could talk well, and the young girl listened to him with lightly parted lips, never taking her eyes from his face.

And he . . . the longer he looked at her the more his heart was overcome by a sweet and tender melancholy—sympathy for himself, pleasure in her, in this new Lenotchka, and a quiet thankfulness to the elder one. It was this very feeling for which he had thirsted in Moscow, but clearer, brighter, purified from all self-love.

When the young girl went off to look at the Kherson monastery he took the elder Lenotchka's hand and kissed it gently.

" Life is wise, and we must submit to her laws,"
he said thoughtfully. " But life is beautiful too. It
is an eternal rising from the dead. You and I will
pass away and vanish out of sight, but from our
bodies, from our thoughts and actions, from our minds,
our inspiration and our talents, there will arise, as
from our ashes, a new Lenotchka and a new Kolya
Voznitsin. All is connected, all linked together.
I shall depart and yet I shall also remain. But one
must love Life and follow her guidance. We are all
alive together—the living and the dead."

He bent down once more to kiss her hand, and she
kissed him tenderly on his white-haired brow. They
looked at one another, and their eyes were wet with
tears ; they smiled gently, sadly, tenderly.

THE IDIOT

WE were seated in a little park, driven there by the unbearable heat of the noonday sun. It was much cooler there than in the streets, where the paving stones, steeped in the rays of the July sun, burnt the soles of one's feet, and the walls of the buildings seemed red-hot. The fine scorching dust of the roadway did not penetrate through the close border of leafy old limes and spreading chestnuts, the latter with their long upright pyramids of rosy flowers looking like gigantic imperial candelabra. The park was full of frolicsome well-dressed children, the older ones playing with hoops and skipping-ropes, chasing one another or going together in pairs, their arms entwined as they walked about with an air of importance, stepping quickly upon the sidewalk. The little ones played at choosing colours, " My lady sent me a hundred roubles," and " King of the castle." And then a group of all the smallest ones gathered together on a large heap of warm yellow sand, moulding it into buckwheat cakes and Easter loaves. The nurses stood round in groups, gossiping about their masters and mistresses ; the governesses sat stiffly upright on the benches, deep in their reading or their needlework.

Suddenly the children stopped their playing and

began to gaze intently in the direction of the entrance gate. We also turned to look. A tall bearded peasant was wheeling in before him a bath-chair in which sat a pitiful helpless being, a boy of about eighteen or twenty years, with a flabby pale face, thick, wet, crimson hanging lips, and the appearance of an idiot. The bearded peasant pushed the chair past us and disappeared down a side path. I noticed as he passed that the enormous sharp-pointed head of the boy moved from side to side, and that at each movement of the chair it fell towards his shoulder or dropped helplessly in front of him.

" Poor man ! " exclaimed my companion in a gentle voice.

I heard such deep and sincere sympathy in his words that I involuntarily looked at him in astonishment. I had known Zimina for a long time—he was a strong, good-natured, jolly, virile type of man serving in one of the regiments quartered in our town. To tell the truth, I shouldn't have expected from him such sincere compassion towards a stranger's misfortune.

" Poor, of course he is, but I shouldn't call him a man," said I, wishing to get into conversation with Zimina.

" Why wouldn't you ? " asked he in his turn.

" Well, it's difficult to say. But surely it's clear to everybody. . . . An idiot has none of the higher impulses and virtues which distinguish man from the animal . . . no reason or speech or will. . . . A dog or a cat possesses these qualities in a much higher degree. . . ."

But Zimina interrupted me.

" Pardon me, please," said he. " I am deeply convinced, on the contrary, that idiots are not lacking in human instincts. These instincts are only clouded over . . . they exist deep below their animal feelings. . . . You see, I once had an experience which gives me, I think, the right to say this. The remembrance of it will never leave me, and every time I see such an afflicted person I feel touched almost to tears. . . . If you'll allow me, I'll tell you why the sight of an idiot moves me to such compassion."

I hastened to beg him to tell his story, and he began.

" In the year 18—, in the early autumn, I went to Petersburg to sit for an examination at the Academy of the General Staff. I stopped in the first hotel I came to, at the corner of Nevsky Prospect and the Fontanka. From my windows I could see the bronze horses on the parapet of the Anitchka Bridge—they were always wet and gleaming as if they had been covered over with new oilcloth. I often drew them on the marble window-seats of my room.

" Petersburg struck me as an unpleasant place, it seemed to be always enveloped in a melancholy grey veil of drizzling rain. But when I went into the Academy for the first time I was overwhelmed and overawed by its grandeur. I remember now its immense broad staircase with marble balustrades, its high-roofed amphilades, its severely proportioned lecture-hall, and its waxed parquet floor, gleaming like a mirror, upon which my provincial feet stepped warily. There were four hundred officers there that day. Against the modest background of green Armenian uniforms there flashed the clattering swords of the Cuirassiers, the scarlet breasts of the Lancers, the white jackets of the Cavalry Guards, waving plumes, the gold of eagles on helmets, the various colours of facings, the silver of swords. These officers were all my rivals, and as I watched them in pride and agitation I pulled at the place where I supposed my moustache would grow by and by. When a busy colonel of the General Staff, with his portfolio under his arm, hurried past us, we shy foot soldiers stepped on one side with reverent awe.

" The examination was to last over a month. I knew no one in all Petersburg, and in the evening, returning to my lodging, I experienced the dulness and wearisomeness of solitude. It was no good talking to any of my companions ; they were all immersed in sines and tangents, in the qualities determining good positions for a battle ground, in calculations about the declination of a projectile. Suddenly I remembered that my father had advised me to seek out in Petersburg our distant relative, Alexandra Ivanovna Gratcheva, and go and visit her. I got a directory, found her address, and set out for a place somewhere on the Gorokhavaya. After some little difficulty I found Alexandra Ivanovna's room ; she was living in her sister's house.

" I opened the door and stood there, hardly seeing anything at first. A stout woman was standing with her back to me, near the single small window of dull green glass. She was bending over a smoky paraffin stove. The room was filled with the odour of paraffin and burning fat. The woman turned round and saw me, and from a corner a barefooted boy, wearing a loose-belted blouse, jumped up and ran quickly towards me. I looked closely at him, and saw at once that he was an idiot, and, though I did not recoil before him, in reality there was a feeling in my heart like that of fear. The idiot looked unintelligently at me, uttering strange sounds, something like *oorli, oorli, oorli.* . . .

" ' Don't be afraid, he won't touch it,' said the woman to the idiot, coming forward. And then to me—' What can I do for you ? ' she added.

" I gave my name and reminded her of my father. She was glad to see me, her face brightened up, she exclaimed in surprise and began to apologise for not having the room in order. The idiot boy came closer to me, and cried out more loudly, *oorli, oorli.* . . .

" ' This is my boy, he's been like that from birth,' said Alexandra Ivanovna with a sad smile. ' What of it. . . . It's the will of God. His name is Stepan.'

" Hearing his name the idiot cried out in a shrill, bird-like voice :

" ' *Papan !* '

" Alexandra Ivanovna patted him caressingly on the shoulder.

" ' Yes, yes, Stepan, Stepan. . . . You see, he guessed we were speaking about him and so he introduced himself.'

" ' *Papan !* ' cried the idiot again, turning his eyes first on his mother and then on me.

" In order to show some interest in the boy I said to him, ' How do you do, Stepan,' and took him by the hand. It was cold, puffy, lifeless. I felt a certain aversion, and only out of politeness went on :

" ' I suppose he's about sixteen.'

" ' Oh, no,' answered the mother. ' Everybody thinks he's about sixteen, but he's over twenty-nine. . . . His beard and moustache have never grown.'

" We talked together. Alexandra Ivanovna was a quiet, timid woman, weighed down by need and misfortune. Her sharp struggle against poverty had entirely killed all boldness of thought in her and all interest in anything outside the narrow bounds of this struggle. She complained to me of the high price of meat, and about the impudence of the cab drivers ; told me of some people who had won money in a lottery, and envied the happiness of rich people. All the time of our conversation Stepan kept his eyes fixed on me. He was apparently struck by and interested in my military overcoat. Three times he put out his hand stealthily to touch the shining buttons, but drew it back each time as if he were afraid.

" ' Is it possible your Stepan cannot say even one word ? ' I asked.

" Alexandra Ivanovna shook her head sadly.

" ' No, he can't speak. He has a few words of his own, but they're not really words—just mutterings. For example, he calls himself *Papan ;* when he wants something to eat he says *mnya ;* he calls money *teki.* Stepan,' she continued, turning to her son, ' where is your *teki ;* show us your *teki.*'

" Stepan jumped up quickly from his chair, ran into a dark corner, and crouched down on his heels. I heard the jingling of some copper coins and the boy's voice saying *oorli, oorli,* but this time in a growling, threatening tone.

" ' He's afraid,' explained the mother ; ' though he doesn't understand what money is, he won't let anyone touch it . . . he won't even let me. . . . Well, well, we won't touch your money, we won't touch it,' she went to her son and soothed him. . . .

" I began to visit them frequently. Stepan interested me, and an idea came to me to try and cure him according to the system of a certain Swiss doctor, who tried to cure his feeble-minded patients by the slow road of logical development. ' He has a few weak impressions of ¦the outer world and of the connection between phenomena,' I thought. ' Can one not combine two or three of these ideas, and so give a fourth, a fifth, and so on? Is it not possible by persistent exercise to strengthen and broaden this poor mind a little ? '

" I brought him a doll dressed as a coachman. He was much pleased with it, and laughed and exclaimed, showing the doll and saying *Papan!* The doll, however, seemed to awaken some doubt in his mind, and that same evening Stepan, who was usually well-disposed to all that was small and weak, tried to break the doll's head on the floor. Then I brought him pictures, tried to interest him in boxes of bricks, and talked to him, naming the different objects and pointing them out to him. But either the Swiss doctor's system was not a good one or I didn't know how to put it into practice—Stepan's development seemed to make no progress at all.

" He was very fond of me in those days. When I came to visit them he ran to meet me, uttering rapturous cries. He never took his eyes off me, and when I ceased to pay him special attention he came up and licked my hands, my shoes, my uniform, just like a dog. When I went away he stood at the window for a long time, and cried so pitifully that the other lodgers in the house complained of him to the landlady.

" But my personal affairs were in a bad way. I failed at the examination, failed unusually badly in the last but one examination in fortifications. Nothing remained but to collect my belongings and go back to my regiment. I don't think that in all my life I shall ever forget that dreadful moment when, coming out of the lecture-hall, I walked across the great vestibule of the Academy. Good Lord ! I felt so small, so pitiful and so humbled, walking down those broad steps covered with grey felt carpet, having a crimson stripe at the side and a white linen tread down the middle.

" It was necessary to get away as quickly as possible. I was urged to this by financial considerations—in my purse I had only ten copecks and one ticket for a dinner at a student's restaurant.

" I thought to myself : ' I must get my " dismissal " quickly and set out at once. Oh, the irony of that word " dismissal." ' But it seemed the most difficult thing in the world. From the Chancellor of the Academy I was sent to the General Staff, thence to the Commandant's office, then to the local intendant, then back to the Academy, and at last to the Treasury. All these places were open only at special times : some from nine to twelve, some from three to five. I was late at all of them, and my position began to appear critical.

" When I used my dinner ticket I had thoughtlessly squandered my ten copecks also. Next day, when I felt the pangs of hunger, I resolved to sell my text-books. Thick ' Baron Bego,' adapted by Bremiker, bound, I sold for twenty-five copecks ; ' Professor Lobko ' for twenty; solid ' General Durop ' no one would buy.

" For two days I was half starved. On the third day there only remained to me three copecks. I screwed up my courage and went to ask a loan from some of my companions, but they all excused themselves by saying there was a Torricellian vacuum in their pockets, and only one acknowledged having a few roubles, but he never lent money. As he explained, with a gentle smile, ' " Loan oft loses both itself and friend," as Shakspeare says in one of his immortal works.'

" Three copecks ! I indulged in tragic reflections. Should I spend them all at once on a box of ten cigarettes, or should I wait until my hunger became unbearable, and then buy bread ?

" How wise I was to decide on the latter ! Towards evening I was as hungry as Robinson Crusoe on his island, and I went out on to the Nevsky Prospect. Ten times I passed and repassed Philipof's the baker's, devouring with my eyes the immense loaves of bread in the windows. Some had yellow crust, some red, and some were strewn with poppy-seed. At last I resolved to go in. Some schoolboys stood there eating hot pies, holding them in scraps of grey greasy paper. I felt a hatred against them for their good fortune.

" ' What would you like ? ' asked the shopman.

" I put on an indifferent air, and answered superciliously :

" ' Cut me off a pound of black bread. . . .'

" I was far from being at my ease while the man skilfully cut the bread with his broad knife. And suddenly I thought to myself : ' Suppose it's more than two and a half copecks a pound, what shall I

do if the man cuts it overweight ? I know it's possible
to owe five or ten roubles in a restaurant, and say to
the waiter, " Put it down to my account, please,"
but what can one do if one hasn't enough by *one*
copeck ? '

" Hurrah ! The bread cost exactly three copecks.
I shifted about from one foot to another while it was
being wrapped up in paper. As soon as I got out of
the shop and felt in my pocket the soft warmth of the
bread, I wanted to cry out for joy and begin to munch
it, as children do those crusts which they steal from
the table after a long day's romping, to eat as they
lie in their beds. And I couldn't restrain myself.
Even in the street I thrust into my mouth two large
tasty morsels.

" Yes. I tell you all this in almost a cheerful tone.
But I was far from cheerful then. Add to my torture
of hunger the stinging shame of failure ; the near
prospect of being the laughing-stock of my regimental
companions ; the charming amiability of the official
on whom depended my cursed ' dismissal.' . . .
I tell you frankly, in those days I was face to face all
the time with the thought of suicide.

" Next day my hunger again seemed unbearable.
I went along to Alexandra Ivanovna. As soon as
Stepan saw me he went into an ecstasy. He cried
out, jumped about me, and licked my coat-sleeve.
When at length I sat down he placed himself near me
on the floor and pressed up against my legs. Alexandra
Ivanovna was obliged to send him away by force.

" It was very unpleasant to have to ask a loan
from this poor woman, who herself found life so
difficult, but I resolved I must do so.

" ' Alexandra Ivanovna,' said I. ' I've nothing to eat. Lend me what money you can, please.'

" She wrung her hands.

" ' My dear boy, I haven't a copeck. Yesterday I pawned my brooch. . . . To-day I was able to buy something in the market, but to-morrow I don't know what I shall do.'

" ' Can't you borrow a little from your sister ? ' I suggested.

" Alexandra Ivanovna looked round with a frightened air, and whispered, almost in terror :

" ' What are you saying ? What ! Don't you know I live here on her charity ? No, we'd better think of some other way of getting it.'

" But the more we thought the more difficult it appeared. After a while we became silent. Evening came on, and the room was filled with a heavy wearisome gloom. Despair and hate and hunger tortured me. I felt as if I were abandoned on the edge of the world, alone and humiliated.

" Suddenly something touched my side. I turned. It was Stepan. He held out to me on his palm a little pile of copper money, and said : ' *Teki, teki, teki.* . . .'

" I did not understand. Then he threw his money on to my knee, called out once more—*teki*—and ran off into his corner.

" Well, why should I hide it ? I wept like a child ; sobbed out, long and loudly. Alexandra Ivanovna wept also, out of pity and tenderness, and from his far corner Stepan uttered his pitiful, unmeaning cry of *oorli, oorli, oorli.*

" When I became quieter I felt better. The

unexpected sympathy of the idiot boy had suddenly warmed and soothed my heart, and shown me that it is possible to live, and that one ought to live, as long as there is love and compassion in the world."

"That is why," concluded Zimina, finishing his story, "that is why I pity all these unfortunates, and why I can't deny that they are human beings." Yes, and by the way, his sympathy brought me happiness. Now I'm very glad I didn't become a "moment"—that's our nickname for the officers of the General Staff. Since that time I have had a full and broad life, and promises to be as full in the future. I'm superstitious about it.

V

THE PICTURE

I

ONE evening, at the house of a well-known literary man, after supper, there arose among the company an unusually heated discussion as to whether there could exist in this time of ours, so barren of exalted feelings, a lasting and unalterable friendship. Everyone said that such friendship did not exist; that there were many trials which the friendship of our days was quite unable to support. It was in the statement of the causes through which friendship was broken, that the company disagreed. One said that money stood in the way of friendship; another that woman stood in the way; a third, similarity of character; a fourth, the cares of family life, and so on.

When the talking and shouting had died down, and the people were tired, though nothing had been explained and no conclusion arrived at, one respected guest, who till that moment had not taken part in the discussion, suddenly broke silence and took up the conversation.

" Yes, gentlemen, all that you have said is both weighty and remarkable. Still I could give you an example from life where friendship triumphed over all the obstacles which you have mentioned, and remained inviolate."

" And do you mean," asked the host, " that this friendship endured to the grave ? "

" No, not to the grave. But it was broken off for a special reason."

" What sort of a reason ? " asked the host.

" A very simple reason, and at the same time an astonishing one. The friendship was broken by St. Barbara."

None of the company could understand how, in our commercial days, St. Barbara could sever a friendship, and they all begged Afanasy Silitch—for such was the respected man's name—to explain his enigmatical words.

Afanasy Silitch smiled as he answered :

" There's nothing enigmatical about the matter. It's a simple and sad story, the story of the suffering of a sick heart. And if you would really like to hear, I'll tell you about it at once with pleasure."

Everyone prepared to listen, and Afanasy Silitch began his tale.

II

In the beginning of the present century there was a family of princes, Belokon Belonogof, famous on account of their illustrious birth, their riches and their pride. But fate destined this family to die out, so that now there is hardly any remembrance of them. The last of these princes, and he was not of the direct line, finished his worldly career quite lately in the Arzhansky, a well-known night house and gambling den in Moscow, among a set of drunkards, wastrels and thieves. But my story is not about him, but about Prince Andrey Lvovitch, with whom the direct line ended.

During his father's lifetime—this was before the emancipation of the serfs—Prince Andrey had a commission in the Guards, and was looked upon as one of the most brilliant officers. He had plenty of money, was handsome, and a favourite with the ladies, a good dancer, a duellist—and what not besides? But when his father died, Prince Andrey threw up his commission in spite of all entreaties from his comrades to remain. "No," said he, "I shall be lost among you, and I'm curious to know all that fate has in store for me."

He was a strange man, of peculiar and, one might say, fantastic habits. He flattered himself that his every dream could at once be realised. As soon as he had buried his father he took himself off abroad. Astonishing to think of the places he went to! Money was sent to him through every agency and banking house, now in Paris, now in Calcutta, then in New York, then Algiers. I know all this on unimpeachable authority, I must tell you, because my father was the chief steward of his estate of two hundred thousand desiatines.[1]

After four years the prince returned, thin, his face overgrown with a beard and brown from sunburn— it was difficult to recognise him. As soon as he arrived he established himself on his estate at Pneestcheva. He went about in his dressing-gown. He found it very dull on the whole.

I was always welcome in his house at that time, for the prince liked my cheerful disposition, and as I had received some sort of education I could be somewhat of a companion to him. And then again,

[1] A desiatin is 2·7 acres.

I was a free person, for my father had been ransomed in the old prince's time.

The prince always greeted me affectionately, and made me sit down with him. He even treated me to cigars. I soon got used to sitting down in his presence, but I could never accustom myself to smoking the cigars—they always gave me a kind of sea-sickness.

I was very curious to see all the things which the prince had brought back with him from his travels. Skins of lions and tigers, curved swords, idols, stuffed animals of all kinds, precious stones and rich stuffs. The prince used to lie on his enormous divan and smoke, and though he laughed at my curiosity he would explain everything I asked about. Then, if he could get himself into the mood, he would begin to talk of his adventures until, as you may well believe, cold shivers ran down my back. He would talk and talk, and then all at once would frown and become silent. I would be silent also. And then he would say, all of a sudden:

" It's dull for me, Afanasy. See, I've been all round the world and seen everything ; I've caught wild horses in Mexico and hunted tigers in India ; I've journeyed on the sea and been in danger of drowning ; I've crossed deserts and been buried in sand—what more is there for me ? Nothing, I say ; there's nothing new under the sun."

I said to him once, quite simply, ' You might get married, prince."

But he only laughed.

" I might marry if I could find the woman whom I could love and honour. I've seen all nations and all classes of women, and since I'm not ugly, not stupid, and I'm a rich man, they have all shown me special attention, but I've never seen the sort of woman that I need. All of them were either mercenary or depraved, or stupid or just a little too much given to good works. But the fact remains, that I feel bored with life. It would be another matter if I had any sort of talent or gift."

And to this I generally used to answer : " But what more talent do you want, prince ? Thank God for your good looks, for your land—which, as you say yourself, is more than belongs to any German prince—and for the powers with which God has blessed you. I shouldn't ask for any other talent."

The prince laughed at this, and said : " You're a stupid, Afanasy, and much too young as yet. Live a little longer, and if you don't become an utter scoundrel, you'll remember these words of mine."

III

Prince Andrey had, however, a gift of his own, in my opinion, a very great gift, for painting, which had been evident even in his childhood. During his stay abroad he had lived for nearly a year in Rome, and had there learnt to paint pictures. He had even thought at one time, he told me, that he might become a real artist, but for some reason he had given up the idea, or he had become idle. Now he was living on his estate at Pneestcheva, he called to mind his former occupation and took to painting pictures again. He painted the river, the mill, an ikon of St. Nicholas for the church—and painted them very well.

Besides this occupation the prince had one other diversion—bear hunting. In our neighbourhood there were a fearful number of these animals. He always went as a mouzhik, with hunting pole and knife, and only took with him the village hunter Nikita Dranny. They called him Dranny because on one occasion a bear had torn a portion of his scalp from his skull, and his head had remained ragged ever since.[1]

With the peasants the prince was quite simple and friendly. He was so easy to approach that if a man wanted wood for his cottage, or if his horse had had an accident, all he had to do was to go straight to the prince and ask for what he wanted. He knew that he would not be refused. The only things the prince could not stand were servility and lying. He never forgave a lie.

And, moreover, the serfs loved him because he made no scandals with their women folk. The maids of our countryside had a name for their good looks, and there were landowners in those days who lived worse than Turks, with a harem for themselves and for their friends. But with us, no—no, nothing of that sort. That is, of course, nothing scandalous. There were occasions, as there always must be, man being so weak, but these were quiet and gentle affairs of the heart, and no one was offended.

But though Prince Andrey was simple and friendly towards his inferiors, he was proud and insolent in his bearing towards his equals and to those in authority, even needlessly so. He especially disliked officials. Sometimes an official would come to our estate to see about the farming arrangements, or in connection with the police or with the excise department—at that time the nobility reckoned any kind of service,

---

[1] "Dranny," means torn or ragged.

except military service, as a degradation—and he would act as a person new to office sometimes does : he would strut about with an air of importance, and ask " Why aren't things *so* and *so ?* " The steward would inform him politely that everything was in accordance with the prince's orders and mustn't be altered. That meant, of course—You take your regulation bribe and be off with you. But the official would not be daunted. " And what's your prince to me ? " he would say. " I'm the representative of the law here." And he would order the steward to take him at once to the prince. My father would warn him out of pity. " Our prince," he would say, " has rather a heavy hand." But the official would not listen. " Where is the prince ? " he would cry. And he would rush into the prince's presence exclaiming, " Mercy on us, what's all this disorder on your estate ! Where else can one see such a state of things ? I . . . we . . ." The prince would let him go on, and say nothing, then suddenly his face would become purple and his eyes would flash—he was terrible to look at when he was angry. " Take the scoundrel to the stables ! " he would cry. And then the official would naturally receive a flogging. At that time many landowners approved of this, and for some reason or other the floggings always took place in the stables, according to the custom of their ancestors. But after two or three days the prince would secretly send my father into the town with a packet of bank-notes for the official who had been chastised. I used to dare to say to him sometimes, " You know, prince, the official will complain about you, and you'll have to answer for your doings." And he would say :

" Well, how can that be ? Let me be brought to account before God and my Emperor, but I'm bound to punish impudence."

But better than this, if you please, was his behaviour towards the Governor at one time. One day a workman from the ferry came running up to him to tell him that the Governor was on the other side of the river.

" Well, what of it ? " said the prince.

" He wants the ferry-boat, your Excellency," said the peasant. He was a sensible man, and knew the prince's character.

" How did he ask for it ? " said the prince.

" The captain of the police sent to say that the ferry-boat was wanted immediately."

The prince at once gave the order :

" Don't let him have it."

And he didn't. Then the Governor guessed what had happened, and he wrote a little note and sent it, asking dear Andrey Lvovitch—they were really distant cousins—to be so kind as to let him use the ferry, and signing the note simply with his Christian and surname. On this the prince himself kindly went down to the river to meet the Governor, and gave him such a feast in welcome that he couldn't get away from Pneestcheva for a whole week.

To people of his own class, even to the most impoverished of them, the prince never refused to " give satisfaction " in cases where a misunderstanding had arisen. But people were generally on their guard, knowing his indomitable character and that he had fought in his time eighteen duels. Duels among the aristocracy were very common at that time.

IV

The prince lived in this way on his estate at Pneest-cheva for more than two years. Then the Tsar sent out his manifesto granting freedom to the serfs, and there commenced a time of alarm and disturbance among the landowners. Many of them were not at all pleased about it, and sat at home on their far-away estates and took to writing reports on the matter. Others, more avaricious and far-sighted, were on the watch with the freed peasants, trying to turn everything to their own advantage. And some were very much afraid of a rising of the peasants, and applied to the authorities for any kind of troops to defend their estates.

When the manifesto arrived, Prince Andrey called his peasants together and explained the matter to them in very simple words, without any insinuations. " You," he said, " are now free, as free as I am. And this is a good thing to have happened. But don't use your freedom to do wrong, because the authorities will always keep an eye on you. And, remember, that as I have helped you in the past I shall continue to do so. And take as much land as you can cultivate for your ransom."

Then he suddenly left the place and went off to Petersburg.

I think you know very well what happened at that time, gentlemen, both in Moscow and in Petersburg. The aristocracy turned up immediately, with piles of money, and went on the spree. The farmers and the holders of concessions and the bankers had amazed all Russia, but they were only as children or puppies in comparison with the landowners. It's terrible to think what took place. Many a time a man's whole fortune was thrown to the winds for one supper.

Prince Andrey fell into this very whirlpool, and began to whirl about. Added to that, he fell in again with his old regimental friends, and then he let himself go altogether. However, he didn't stay long in Petersburg, for he was quickly forced to leave the city against his will. It was all because of some horses.

V

He was having supper one evening with his officer friends in one of the most fashionable restaurants. They had had very much to drink, champagne above all. Suddenly the talk turned on horses—it's well known to be an eternal subject of conversation with officers— as to who owned the most spirited team in Petersburg. One Cossack—I don't remember his name, I only know that he was one of the reigning princes in the Caucasus—said that at that time the most spirited horses were a pair of black stallions belonging to ——, and he named a lady in an extremely high position.

" They are not horses," said he, " but wild things. It's only Ilya who can manage them, and they won't allow themselves to be out-distanced."

But Prince Andrey laughed at this.

" I'd pass them with my bays."

" No, you wouldn't," said the Cossack.

" Yes, I would."

" You wouldn't race them."

" Yes, I would."

" Well, in that case," said the Cossack, " we'll lay a wager about it at once."

And the wager was laid. It was agreed that if Prince Andrey were put to shame he should give the Cossack his pair of bay horses, and with them a sledge and a carriage with silver harness, and if the prince got in front of Ilya's team, then the Cossack would buy up all the tickets in the theatre for an opera when Madame Barba was to sing, so that they could walk about in the gallery and not allow anyone else in the theatre. At that time Madame Barba had captivated all the *beau-monde*.

Very well, then. On the next day, when the prince woke up, he ordered the bay horses to be put into the carriage. The horses were not very much to look at, hairy country horses, but they were sufficiently fast goers ; the most important thing about them was that they liked to get in front of other horses, and they were exceptionally long-winded.

As soon as his companions saw that the prince was really in earnest about the matter, they tried to dissuade him. " Give up this wager," urged they, " you can't escape getting into some trouble over it." But the prince would not listen, and ordered his coachman, Bartholomew, to be called.

The coachman, Bartholomew, was a gloomy and, so to speak, absent-minded man. God had endowed him with such extraordinary strength that he could even stop a troika when the horses were going at full gallop. The horses would fall back on their hind legs. He drank terribly, had no liking for conversation with anyone, and, though he adored the prince with all his soul, he was rude and supercilious towards him, so that he sometimes had to receive a flogging. The prince called Bartholomew to him and said : " Do you think, Bartholomew, you could race another pair of horses with our bays ? "

" Which pair ? " asked Bartholomew.

The prince told him which horses they were. Bartholomew scratched the back of his head.

" I know that pair," he said, " and I know Ilya, their driver, pretty well. He's a dangerous man. However, if your Excellency wishes it, we can race them. Only, if the bay horses are ruined, don't be angry."

" Very well," said the prince. " And now, how much vodka shall we pour down your throat ? "

But Bartholomew wouldn't have any vodka.

" I can't manage the horses if I'm drunk," said he.

The prince got in the carriage, and they started. They took up their position at the end of the Nevsky Prospect, and waited. It was known beforehand that the important personage would drive out at midday. And so it happened. At twelve o'clock the pair of black horses were seen. Ilya was driving, and the lady was in the sledge.

The prince let them just get in front, and then he said to the coachman :

" Drive away ! "

Bartholomew let the horses go. As soon as Ilya heard the tramping of the horses behind, he turned round ; the lady looked round also. Ilya gave his horses the reins, and Bartholomew also whipped up his. But the owner of the blacks was a woman of an ardent and fearless temperament, and she had a passion for horses. She said to Ilya, " Don't dare to let that scoundrel pass us ! "

What began to happen then I can't describe. Both the coachmen and the horses were as if mad; the snow rose up above them in clouds as they raced along. At first the blacks seemed to be gaining, but they couldn't last out for a long time, they got tired. The prince's horses went ahead. Near the railway station, Prince Andrey jumped out of his carriage, and the personage threatened him angrily with her finger.

Next day the governor of Petersburg—His Serene Highness Prince Suvorof—sent for the prince, and said to him:

"You must leave Petersburg at once, prince. If you're not punished and made an example of, it's only because the lady whom you treated in such a daring fashion yesterday has a great partiality for bold and desperate characters. And she knows also about your wager. But don't put your foot in Petersburg again, and thank the Lord that you've got off so cheaply."

But, gentlemen, I've been gossiping about Prince Andrey and I haven't yet touched on what I promised to tell you. However, I'm soon coming to the end of my story. And, though it has been in rather a disjointed fashion, I have described the personality of the prince as best I can.

VI

After his famous race the prince went off to Moscow, and there continued to behave as he had done in Petersburg, only on a larger scale. At one time the whole town talked of nothing but his caprices. And it was there that something happened to him which caused all the folks at Pneestcheva to mock. A woman came into his life.

But I must tell you what sort of a woman she was. A queen of women! There are none like her in these days. Of a most marvellous beauty. . . . She had formerly been an actress, then she had married a merchant millionaire, and when he died—she didn't want to marry anyone else—she said that she preferred to be free.

What specially attracted the prince to her was her carelessness. She didn't wish to know anyone, neither rich nor illustrious people, and she seemed to think nothing of her own great wealth. As soon as Prince Andrey saw her he fell in love with her. He was used to having women run after him, and so he had very little respect for them. But in this case the lady paid him no special attention at all. She was gay and affable, she accepted his bouquets and his presents, but directly he spoke of his feelings she laughed at him. The prince was stung by this treatment. He nearly went out of his mind.

Once the prince went with Marya Gavrilovna— that was the lady's name—to the *Yar*, to hear some gipsy singers. The party numbered fifteen. At that time the prince was surrounded and fawned upon by a whole crowd of hangers-on—his Belonogof company, as he called them—his own name was Belonogof. They were all seated at a table drinking wine, and the gipsies were singing and dancing. Suddenly, Marya Gavrilovna wanted to smoke. She took a *packetoska*—the sort of twisted straw cigarette they used to smoke in those days—and looked round for a light. The prince noticed this, and in a moment he pulled out a bank-note for a thousand roubles, lighted it at a candle and handed it to her. Everybody in the company exclaimed; the gipsies even stopped singing, and their eyes gleamed with greed. And then someone at a neighbouring table said, not very loudly, but with sufficient distinctness, " Fool ! "

The prince jumped up as if he had been shot. At the other table sat a small sickly-looking man, who looked straight at the prince in the calmest manner possible. The prince went over to him at once.

" How dare you call me a fool ? Who are you ? "

The little man regarded him very coolly.

" I," said he, " am the artist Rozanof. And I called you a fool because, with that money you burnt just to show off, you might have paid for the support of four sick people in the hospital for a whole year."

Everybody sat and waited for what would happen. The unrestrained character of the prince was well known. Would he at once chastise the little man, or call him out to a duel, or simply order him to be whipped ?

But, after a little silence, the prince suddenly turned to the artist with these unexpected words :

" You're quite right, Mr. Rozanof. I did indeed act as a fool before this crowd. But now if you don't at once give me your hand, and accept five thousand roubles for the Marinskaya Hospital, I shall be deeply offended."

And Rozanof answered: " I'll take the money, and I'll give you my hand with equal pleasure."

Then Marya Gavrilovna whispered to the prince, " Ask the artist to come and talk to us, and send away these friends of yours."

The prince turned politely to Rozanof and begged him to join them, and then he turned to the officers and said, " Be off with you ! "

VII

From that time the prince and Rozanof were bound together in a close friendship. They couldn't spend a day without seeing one another. Either the artist came to visit the prince or Prince Andrey went to see the artist. Rozanof was living then in two rooms on the fourth floor of a house in Mestchanskaya Street —one he used as a studio, the other was his bedroom. The prince invited the artist to come and live with him, but Rozanof refused. " You are very dear to me," said he, " but in wealthy surroundings I might be idle and forget my art." So he wouldn't make any change.

They were interested in everything that concerned one another. Rozanof would begin to talk of painting, of various pictures, of the lives of great artists—and the prince would listen and not utter a word. Then afterwards he would tell about his adventures in wild countries, and the artist's eyes would glisten.

" Wait a little," he would say. " I think I shall soon paint a great picture. Then I shall have plenty of money, and we'll go abroad together."

" But why do you want money ? " asked the prince. " If you like, we can go to-morrow. Everything I have I will share with you."

But the artist remained firm.

" No, wait a little," said he. " I'll paint the picture and then we can talk about it."

There was a real friendship between them. It

was even marvellous — for Rozanof had such an influence over the prince that he restrained him from many of the impetuous and thoughtless actions to which, with his fiery temperament, he was specially prone.

VIII

The prince's love for Marya Gavrilovna did not become less, it even increased in fervency, but he had no success with the lady. He pressed his hands to his heart, and went down on his knees to her many times, but she had only one answer for him: " But what can I do if I don't love you ? " " Well, don't love me," said the prince; " perhaps you will love me by and by, but I can't be happy without you." Then she would say, " I'm very sorry for you, but I can't help your unhappiness." " You love someone else, perhaps," said the prince. " Perhaps I love someone else," said she, and she laughed.

The prince grew very sad about it. He would lie at home on the sofa, gloomy and silent, turn his face to the wall, and even refuse to take any food. Everybody in the house went about on tip-toe. . . . One day Rozanof called when the prince was in this state, and he too looked out of sorts. He came into the prince's room, said " Good morning," and nothing more. They were both silent. At length the artist pulled himself together and said to the prince, " Listen, Andrey Lvovitch. I'm very sorry that with my friendly hand I have got to deal you a blow."

The prince, who was lying with his face to the wall, said, " Please come straight to the point without any introduction."

Then the artist explained what he meant.

"Marya Gavrilovna is going to live with me as my wife," said he.

"You're going out of your mind," said the prince.

"No," said the artist, "I'm not going out of my mind. I have loved Marya Gavrilovna for a long time, but I never dared tell her so. But to-day she said to me : 'Why do we hide things from one another ? I've seen for a long time that you love me, and I also love you. I won't marry you, but we can live together. . . .'"

The artist told the whole story, and the prince lay on the sofa neither moving nor saying a word. Rozanof sat there and looked at him, and presently he went quietly away.

IX

However, after a week, the prince overcame his feelings, though it cost him a good deal, for his hair had begun to turn grey. He went to Rozanof and said :

"I see love can't be forced, but I don't want to lose my only friend for the sake of a woman."

Rozanof put his arms about his friend and wept. And Marya Gavrilovna gave him her hand—she was there at the time—and said :

"I admire you very much, Andrey Lvovitch, and I also want to be your friend."

Then the prince was quite cheered up, and his face brightened. "Confess now," said he, "if Rozanof hadn't called me a fool that time in the Yar, you wouldn't have fallen in love with him ? "

She only smiled.

" That's very probable," said she.

Then, in another week, something else happened. Prince Andrey came in one day, dull and absent-minded. He spoke of one thing and another, but always as if he had some persistent idea in the background. The artist, who knew his character, asked what was the matter.

" Oh, nothing," said the prince.

" Well, but all the same, what is it ? "

" Oh, it's nothing, I tell you. The stupid bank in which my money is . . ."

" Well ? "

" It's failed. And now I've nothing of all my property except what I have here with me."

" Oh, that's really nothing," said Rozanof, and he at once called Marya Gavrilovna, and they had the upper part of their house put in order so that the prince might come and live with them.

x

So the prince settled down to live with Rozanof. He used to lie on the sofa all day, read French novels and polish his nails. But he soon got tired of this, and one day he said to his friend :

" Do you know, I once learnt to paint ! "

Rozanof was surprised. " No, did you ? "

" Yes, I did. I can even show you some of my pictures."

Rozanof looked at them, and then he said :

" You have very good capabilities, but you have been taught in a stupid school."

The prince was delighted.

" Well," he asked, " if I began to study now, do you think I should ever paint anything good ? "

" I think it's very probable indeed."

" Even if I've been an idler up till now ? "

" Oh, that's nothing. You can overcome it by work."

" When my hair is grey ? "

" That doesn't matter either. Other people have begun later than you. If you like, I'll give you lessons myself."

So they began to work together. Rozanof could only marvel at the great gift for painting which the prince displayed. And the prince was so taken up by his work that he never wanted to leave it, and had to be dragged away by force.

Five months passed. Then, one day, Rozanof came to the prince and said :

" Well, my colleague, you are ripening in your art, and you already understand what a drawing is and the school. Formerly you were a savage, but now you have developed a refined taste. Come with me and I will show you the picture I once gave you a hint about. Until now I've kept it a secret from everybody, but now I'll show you, and you can tell me your opinion of it."

He led the prince into his studio, placed him in a corner from whence he could get a good view, and drew a curtain which hung in front of the picture. It represented St. Barbara washing the sores on the feet of lepers.

The prince stood for a long time and looked at the picture, and his face became gloomy as if it had been darkened.

" Well, what do you think of it ? " asked Rozanof.

" This——" answered the prince, with rancour, " that I shall never touch a paint-brush again."

XI

Rozanof's picture was the outcome of the highest inspiration and art. It showed St. Barbara kneeling before the lepers and bathing their terrible feet, her face radiant and joyful, and of an unearthly beauty. The lepers looked at her in prayerful ecstasy and inexpressible gratitude. The picture was a marvel. Rozanof had designed it for an exhibition, but the newspapers proclaimed its fame beforehand. The public flocked to the artist's studio. People came, looked at St. Barbara and the lepers, and stood there for an hour or more. And even those who knew nothing about art were moved to tears. An Englishman, who was in Moscow at the time, a Mr. Bradley, offered fifteen thousand roubles for the picture as soon as he looked at it. Rozanof, however, would not agree to sell it.

But something strange was happening to the prince at that time. He went about with a sullen look, seemed to get thinner, and talked to no one. He took to drink. Rozanof tried to get him to talk, but he only got rude answers, and when the public had left the studio, the prince would seat himself before the easel and remain there for hours, immovable, gazing at the holy Barbara, gazing . . .

So it went on for more than a fortnight, and then something unexpected happened—to tell the truth, something dreadful.

Rozanof came home one day and asked if Prince

Andrey were in. The servant said that the prince had gone out very early that morning, and had left a note.

The artist took the note and read it. And this was what was written. " Forgive my terrible action. I was mad, and in a moment I have repented of my deed. I am going away, never to return, because I haven't strength to kill myself." The note was signed with his name.

Then the artist understood it all. He rushed into his studio and found his divine work lying on the floor, torn to pieces, trampled upon, cut into shreds with a knife. . . .

Then he began to weep, and said :

" I'm not sorry for the picture, but for him. Why couldn't he tell me what was in his mind ? I would have sold the picture at once, or given it away to someone."

But nothing more was ever heard of Prince Andrey, and no one knew how he lived after his mad deed.

VI

HAMLET

I

" HAMLET " was being played.

All tickets had been sold out before the morning of the performance. The play was more than usually attractive to the public because the principal part was to be taken by the famous Kostromsky, who, ten years before, had begun his artistic career with a simple walking-on part in this very theatre, and since then had played in all parts of Russia, and gained a resounding fame such as no other actor visiting the provinces had ever obtained. It was true that, during the last year, people had gossiped about him, and there had even appeared in the Press certain vague and only half-believed rumours about him. It was said that continual drunkenness and debauch had unsettled and ruined Kostromsky's gigantic talent, that only by being " on tour " had he continued to enjoy the fruit of his past successes, that impresarios of the great metropolitan theatres had begun to show less of their former slavish eagerness to agree to his terms. Who knows, there may have been a certain amount of truth in these rumours ? But the name of Kostromsky was still great enough to draw the public. For three days in succession, in spite of the increased prices of seats, there had been a long line of people waiting at the box office. Speculative buyers had resold tickets at three, four, and even five times their original value.

The first scene was omitted, and the stage was being prepared for the second. The footlights had not yet been turned up. The scenery of the queen's palace was hanging in strange, rough, variegated cardboard. The stage carpenters were hastily driving in the last nails.

The theatre had gradually filled with people. From behind the curtain could be heard a dull and monotonous murmur.

Kostromsky was seated in front of the mirror in his dressing-room. He had only just arrived, but was already dressed in the traditional costume of the Danish prince ; black-cloth buckled shoes, short black velvet jacket with wide lace collar. The theatrical barber stood beside him in a servile attitude, holding a wig of long fair hair.

" He is fat and pants for breath," declaimed Kostromsky, rubbing some cold cream on his palm and beginning to smear his face with it.

The barber suddenly began to laugh.

" What's the matter with you, fool ? " asked the actor, not taking his eyes from the mirror.

" Oh, I . . . er . . . nothing . . . er. . . ."

" Well, it's evident you're a fool. They say that I'm too fat and flabby. And Shakspeare himself said that Hamlet was fat and panted for breath. They're all good-for-nothings, these newspaper fellows. They just bark at the wind."

Having finished with the cold cream, Kostromsky

put the flesh tints on to his face in the same manner, but looking more attentively into the mirror.

"Yes, make-up is a great thing; but all the same, my face is not what it used to be. Look at the bags under my eyes, and the deep folds round my mouth . . . cheeks all puffed out . . . nose lost its fine shape. Ah, well, we'll struggle on a bit longer. . . . Kean drank, Mochalof drank . . . hang it all. Let them talk about Kostromsky and say that he's a bloated drunkard. Kostromsky will show them in a moment . . . these youngsters . . . these water-people . . . he'll show them what real talent can do."

"You, Ethiop, have you ever seen me act?" he asked, turning suddenly on the barber.

The man trembled all over with pleasure.

"Mercy on us, Alexander Yevgrafitch. . . . Yes, I . . . O Lord! . . . is it possible for me not to have seen the greatest, one may say, of Russian artists? Why, in Kazan I made a wig for you with my own hands."

"The devil may know you. I don't remember," said Kostromsky, continuing to make long and narrow lines of white down the length of his nose, "there are so many of you. . . . Pour out something to drink!"

The barber poured out half a tumblerful of vodka from the decanter on the marble dressing-table, and handed it to Kostromsky.

The actor drank it off, screwed up his face, and spat on the floor.

"You'd better have a little something to eat, Alexander Yevgrafitch," urged the barber persuasively. "If you take it neat . . . it goes to your head. . . ."

Kostromsky had almost finished his make-up;
he had only to put on a few streaks of brown colouring,
and the " clouds of grief " overshadowed his changed
and ennobled countenance.

" Give me my cloak ! " said he imperiously to the
barber, getting up from his chair.

From the theatre there could already be heard,
in the dressing-room, the sounds of the tuning of the
instruments in the orchestra.

The crowds of people had all arrived. The living
stream could be heard pouring into the theatre and
flowing into the boxes stalls and galleries with the noise
and the same kind of peculiar rumble as of a far-off sea.

" It's a long time since the place has been so full,"
remarked the barber in servile ecstasy; " there's
n-not an empty seat ! "

Kostromsky sighed.

He was still confident in his great talent, still full
of a frank self-adoration and the illimitable pride of
an artist, but, although he hardly dared to allow
himself to be conscious of it, he had an uneasy feeling
that his laurels had begun to fade. Formerly he had
never consented to come to the theatre until the
director had brought to his hotel the stipulated five
hundred roubles, his night's pay, and he had sometimes
taken offence in the middle of a play and gone home,
swearing with all his might at the director, the manager,
and the whole company.

The barber's remark was a vivid and painful reminder
of these years of his extraordinary and colossal
successes. Nowadays no director would bring him
payment in advance, and he could not bring himself
to contrive to demand it.

" Pour out some more vodka," said he to the barber.

There was no more vodka left in the decanter. But the actor had received sufficient stimulus. His eyes, encircled by fine sharp lines of black drawn along both eyelids, were larger and more full of life, his bent body straightened itself, his swollen legs, in their tight-fitting black, looked lithe and strong.

He finished his toilet by dusting powder over his face, with an accustomed hand, then slightly screwing up his eyes he regarded himself in the mirror for the last time, and went out of the dressing-room.

When he descended the staircase, with his slow self-reliant step, his head held high, every movement of his was marked by that easy gracious simplicity which had so impressed the actors of the French company, who had seen him when he, a former draper's assistant, had first appeared in Moscow.

II

The stage manager had already rushed forward to greet Kostromsky.

The lights in the theatre blazed high. The chaotic disharmony of the orchestra tuning their instruments suddenly died down. The noise of the crowd grew louder, and then, as it were, suddenly subsided a little.

Out broke the sounds of a loud triumphal march. Kostromsky went up to the curtain and looked through a little round hole made in it at about a man's height. The theatre was crowded with people. He could only see distinctly the faces of those in the first three rows, but beyond, wherever his eye turned, to left, to right, above, below, there moved, in a sort of bluish haze, an immense number of many-coloured human blobs. Only the side boxes, with their white and gold arabesques and their crimson barriers, stood out against all this agitated obscurity. But as he looked through the little hole in the curtain, Kostromsky did not experience in his soul that feeling—once so familiar and always singularly fresh and powerful— of a joyous, instantaneous uplifting of his whole moral being. It was just a year since he had ceased to feel so, and he explained his indifference by thinking he had grown accustomed to the stage, and did not suspect that this was the beginning of paralysis of his tired and worn-out soul.

The manager rushed on to the stage behind him, all red and perspiring, with dishevelled hair.

" Devil ! Idiocy ! All's gone to the devil ! One might as well cut one's throat," he burst out in a voice of fury, running up to Kostromsky. Here you, devils, let me come to the curtain ! I must go out and tell the people at once that there will be no performance. There's no Ophelia. Understand ! There's no Ophelia."

" How do you mean there's no Ophelia ? " said the astonished Kostromsky, knitting his brows. " You're joking, aren't you, my friend ? "

" There's no joking in me," snarled the manager. " Only just this moment, five minutes before she's wanted, I receive this little *billet-doux* from Milevskaya. Just look, look, what this idiot writes ! ' I'm in bed with a feverish cold and can't play my part.' Well ? Don't you understand what it means ? This is not a pound of raisins, old man, pardon the expression, it means we can't produce the play."

" Someone else must take her place," Kostromsky flashed out. " What have her tricks to do with me ? "

" Who can take her place, do you think ? Bobrova is Gertrude, Markovitch and Smolenskaya have a holiday and they've gone off to the town with some officers. It would be ridiculous to make an old woman take the part of Ophelia. Don't you think so ? Or there's someone else if you like, a young girl student. Shall we ask her ? "

He pointed straight in front of him to a young girl who was just walking on to the stage ; a girl in a modest coat and fur cap, with gentle pale face and large dark eyes.

The young girl, astonished at such unexpected attention, stood still.

" Who is she ? " asked Kostromsky in a low voice, looking with curiosity at the girl's face.

" Her name's Yureva. She's here as a student. She's smitten with a passion for dramatic art, you see," answered the manager, speaking loudly and without any embarrassment.

" Listen to me, Yureva. Have you ever read ' Hamlet' ? " asked Kostromsky, going nearer to the girl.

" Of course I have," answered she in a low confused voice.

" Could you play Ophelia here this evening ? "

" I know the part by heart, but I don't know if I could play it."

Kostromsky went close up to her and took her by the hand.

" You see . . . Milevskaya has refused to play, and the theatre's full. Make up your mind, my dear ! You can be the saving of us all ! "

Yureva hesitated and was silent, though she would have liked to say much, very much, to the famous actor. It was he who, three years ago, by his marvellous acting, had unconsciously drawn her young heart, with an irresistible attraction, to the stage. She had never missed a performance in which he had taken part, and she had often wept at nights after seeing him act in " Cain," in " The Criminal's Home," or in " Uriel da Costa." She would have accounted it her greatest happiness, and one apparently never to be attained . . . not to speak to Kostromsky; no, of that she had never dared to dream, but only to see him nearer in ordinary surroundings.

She had never lost her admiration of him, and only an actor like Kostromsky, spoilt by fame and satiated by the attentions of women, could have failed to notice at rehearsals the two large dark eyes which followed him constantly with a frank and persistent adoration.

" Well, what is it ? Can we take your silence for consent ? " insisted Kostromsky, looking into her face with a searching, kindly glance, and putting into the somewhat nasal tones of his voice that irresistible tone of friendliness which he well knew no woman could withstand.

Yureva's hand trembled in his, her eyelids drooped, and she answered submissively :

" Very well. I'll go and dress at once."

III

The curtain rose, and no sooner did the public see their favourite than the theatre shook with sounds of applause and cries of ecstasy.

Kostromsky standing near the king's throne,

bowed many times, pressed his hand to his heart, and
sent his gaze over the whole assembly.

At length, after several unsuccessful attempts,
the king, taking advantage of a moment when the
noise had subsided a little, raised his voice and began
his speech:

> "Though yet of Hamlet our dear brother's death
> The memory be green, and that it us befitted
> To bear our hearts in grief, and our whole kingdom
> To be contracted in one brow of woe;
> Yet so far hath discretion fought with nature
> That we with wisest sorrow think on him. . . ."

The enthusiasm of the crowd had affected Kostromsky, and when the king turned to him, and
addressed him as "brother and beloved son," the words
of Hamlet's answer:

> "A little more than kin and less than kind,"

sounded so gloomily ironical and sad that an
involuntary thrill ran through the audience.

And when the queen, with hypocritical words of
consolation, said:

> "Thou knowst 'tis common; all that lives must die,
> Passing through nature to eternity,"

he slowly raised his long eyelashes, which he had kept
lowered until that moment, looked reproachfully at
her, and then answered with a slight shake of the head:

> "Ay, madam, it is common."

After these words, expressing so fully his grief
for his dead father, his own aversion from life and sub-
mission to fate, and his bitter scorn of his mother's
light-mindedness, Kostromsky, with the special, delicate,

inexplicable sensitiveness of an experienced actor, felt that now he had entirely gripped his audience and bound them to him with an inviolable chain.

It seemed as if no one had ever before spoken with such marvellous force that despairing speech of Hamlet at the exit of the king and queen :

> "O, that this too too solid flesh would melt,
> Thaw, and resolve itself into a dew ! "

The nasal tones of Kostromsky's voice were clear and flexible. Now it rang out with a mighty clang, then sank to a gentle velvety whisper or burst into hardly restrained sobs.

And when, with a simple yet elegant gesture, Kostromsky pronounced the last words :

> "But break my heart, for I must hold my tongue ! "

the audience roared out its applause.

" Yes, the public and I understand one another," said the actor as he went off the stage into the wings after the first act. " Here, you crocodile, give me some vodka ! " he shouted at once to the barber who was coming to meet him.

IV

" Well, little father, don't you think he's fine ? " said a young actor-student to Yakovlef, the patriarch of provincial actors, who was taking the part of the king.

The two were standing together on the staircase which led from the dressing-rooms to the stage.

Yakovlef pursed and bit his full thick lips.

" Fine ! Fine ! But all the same, he acts as a boy. Those who saw Mochalof play Hamlet wouldn't marvel at this. I, brother, was just such a little chap as you are when I had the happiness of seeing him first. And when I come to die, I shall look back on that as the most blessed moment of my life. When he got up from the floor of the stage and said :

" ' Let the stricken deer go weep '

the audience rose as one man, hardly daring to breathe. And now watch carefully how Kostromsky takes that very scene."

" You're very hard to please, Valerie Nikolaitch."

" Not at all. But you watch him ; to tell you the truth, I can't. Do you think I am watching *him* ? "

" Well, who then ? "

" Ah, brother, look at Ophelia. There's an actress for you ! "

" But Valerie Nikolaitch, she's only a student."

" Idiot ! Don't mind that. You didn't notice how she said the words :

" ' He spoke to me of love, but was so tender,
So timid, and so reverent.' [1]

Of course you didn't. And I've been nearly thirty years on the stage, and I tell you I've never heard anything like it. She's got talent. You mark my words, in the fourth act she'll have such a success that your Kostromsky will be in a fury. You see ! "

[1] Perhaps—" He hath, my lord, of late made many tenders
Of his affection to me."
The Russian lines do not clearly correspond to any of Shakespeare's.—[ED.]

V

The play went on. The old man's prophecy was abundantly fulfilled. The enthusiasm of Kostromsky only lasted out the first act. It could not be roused again by repeated calls before the curtain, by applause, or by the gaze of his enormous crowd of admirers, who thronged into the wings to look at him with gentle reverence. There now remained in him only the very smallest store of that energy and feeling which he had expended with such royal generosity three years ago on every act.

He had wasted his now insignificant store in the first act, when he had been intoxicated by the loud cries of welcome and applause from the public. His will was weakened, his nerves unbraced, and not even increased doses of alcohol could revive him. The imperceptible ties which had connected him with his audience at first were gradually weakening, and, though the applause at the end of the second act was as sincere as at the end of the first, yet it was clear that the people were applauding, not him, but the charm of his name and fame.

Meanwhile, each time she appeared on the stage, Ophelia — Yureva — progressed in favour. This hitherto unnoticed girl, who had previously played only very minor parts, was now, as it were, working a miracle. She seemed a living impersonation of the real daughter of Polonius, a gentle, tender, obedient daughter, with deep hidden feeling and great love in her soul, empoisoned by the venom of grief.

The audience did not yet applaud Yureva, but

they watched her, and whenever she came on the stage the whole theatre calmed down to attention. She herself had no suspicion that she was in competition with the great actor, and taking from him attention and success, and even the spectators themselves were unconscious of the struggle.

The third act was fatal for Kostromsky. His appearance in it was preceded by the short scene in which the king and Polonius agree to hide themselves and listen to the conversation between Hamlet and Ophelia, in order to judge of the real reason of the prince's madness. Kostromsky came out from the wings with slow steps, his hands crossed upon his breast, his head bent low, his stockings unfastened and the right one coming down.

" To be or not to be—that is the question."

He spoke almost inaudibly, all overborne by serious thought, and did not notice Ophelia, who sat at the back of the stage with an open book on her knee.

This famous soliloquy had always been one of Kostromsky's show places. Some years ago, in this very town and this very theatre, after he had finished this speech by his invocation to Ophelia, there had been for a moment that strange and marvellous silence which speaks more eloquently than the noisiest applause. And then everyone in the theatre had gone into an ecstasy of applause, from the humblest person in the back row of the gallery to the exquisites in the private boxes.

Alas, now both Kostromsky himself and his audience remained cold and unmoved, though he was not yet conscious of it.

" Thus conscience does make cowards of us all ;
And thus the native hue of resolution,
Is sicklied o'er with the pale cast of thought
And enterprises of great pith and moment,
With this regard their currents turn awry,
And lose the name of action,"

he went on, gesticulating and changing his intonation
from old memory.   And he thought to himself that
when he saw Ophelia he would go down on his knees
in front of her and say the final words of his speech,
and that the audience would weep and cry out with a
sweet foolishness.

And there was Ophelia.   He turned to the audience
with a cautious warning " Soft you, now ! " and then
walking swiftly across the stage he knelt down and
exclaimed :

" — Nymph, in thy orisons
Be all my sins remember'd,"

and then got up immediately, expecting a burst of
applause.

But there was no applause.   The public were
puzzled, quite unmoved, and all their attention was
turned on Ophelia.

For some seconds he could think of nothing ; it was
only when he heard at his side a gentle girl's voice
asking, " Prince, are you well ? "—a voice which
trembled with the tears of sorrow for a love destroyed—
that, in a momentary flash, he understood all.

It was a moment of awful enlightenment.   Kostromsky recognised it clearly and mercilessly—the indifference of the public ; his own irrevocable past ; the
certainty of the near approach of the end to his noisy
but short-lived fame.

Oh, with what hatred did he look upon this girl,

so graceful, beautiful, innocent, and — tormenting thought—so full of talent. He would have liked to throw himself upon her, beat her, throw her on the ground and stamp with his feet upon that delicate face, with its large dark eyes looking up at him with love and pity. But he restrained himself, and answered in lowered tones :

"I humbly thank you ; well, well, well."

After this scene Kostromsky was recalled, but he heard, much louder than his own name, the shouts from the gallery, full with students, for Yureva, who, however, refused to appear.

VI

The strolling players were playing "The Murder of Gonzago." Kostromsky was half sitting, half lying on the floor opposite to the court, his head on Ophelia's knees. Suddenly he turned his face upward to her, and giving forth an overwhelming odour of spirit, whispered in drunken tones :

"Listen, madam. What's your name ? Listen ! "

She bent down a little towards him, and said in an answering whisper :

"What is it ? "

"What pretty feet you have ! " said he. "Listen ! You must be pretty . . . everywhere."

Yureva turned away her face in silence.

"I mean it, by heaven ! " Kostromsky went on, nothing daunted. "No doubt you have a lover here, haven't you ? "

She made no reply.

Kostromsky wanted to insult her still more, to

hurt her, and her silence was a new irritation to him.

" You have ?   Oh, that's very very foolish of you. Such a face as yours is . . . is your whole capital. . . . You will pardon my frankness, but you're no actress. What are you doing on the stage ? "

Fortunately, it was necessary for him to take part in the acting.   Yureva was left in peace, and she moved a little away from him.   Her eyes filled with tears.   In Kostromsky's face she had seen a spiteful and merciless enemy.

But Kostromsky became less powerful in each scene, and when the act was finished there was very slight applause to gratify him.   But no one else was clapped.

VII

The fourth act commenced.   As soon as Ophelia came on to the stage in her white dress, adorned with flowers and straw, her eyes wide open and staring, a confused murmur ran through the audience, and was followed by an almost painful silence.

And when Ophelia sang her little songs about her dear love, in gentle, naïve tones, there was a strange breathing among the audience as if a deep and general sigh had burst from a thousand breasts :

> " How should I your true love know,
> From another one ?
> By his cockle hat and staff,
> And his sandal shoon."

" Oh, poor Ophelia !   What are you singing ? " asked the queen sympathetically.

The witless eyes of Ophelia were turned on the queen in wonder, as if she had not noticed her before.

" What am I singing ? " she asked in astonishment.
" Listen to my song :

> " ' He is dead and gone, lady,
> He is dead and gone ;
> At his head a grass-green turf,
> At his heels a stone.' "

No one in the theatre could look on with indifference,
all were in the grip of a common feeling, all sat as if
enchanted, never moving their eyes from the stage.

But more persistently, and more eagerly than anyone
else, Kostromsky stood in the wings and watched
her every movement. In his soul, his sick and proud
soul, which had never known restraint or limit to
its own desires and passions, there now blazed a
terrible and intolerable hatred. He felt that this
poor and modest girl-student had definitely snatched
from his hands the evening's success. His drunkenness had, as it were, quite gone out of his head. He
did not yet know how this envious spite which boiled
in him could expend itself, but he awaited impatiently
the time when Ophelia would come off the stage.

" I hope all will be well. We must be patient ; but I cannot
choose but weep to think they should lay him in the cold
ground,"

he heard Ophelia say, in a voice choked with the
madness of grief.

" My brother shall know of it, and so I thank you for your
good counsel. Come, my coach ! Good-night, ladies ; good-
night, sweet ladies ; good-night, good-night."

Yureva came out in the wings, agitated, breathing
deeply, pale even under her make-up. She was
followed by deafening cries from the audience. In
the doorway she stumbled up against Kostromsky.
He purposely made no way for her, but she, even

when her shoulder brushed against his, did not notice him, so excited was she by her acting and the rapturous applause of the public.

" Yureva ! Yureva ! Brav-o-o ! "

She went back and bowed.

As she returned again to the wings she again stumbled against Kostromsky, who would not allow her to pass. Yureva looked at him with a terrified glance, and said timidly :

" Please allow me to pass ! "

" Be more careful please, young person ! " answered he, with malicious haughtiness. " If you are applauded by a crowd of such idiots, it doesn't mean you can push into people with impunity." And seeing her silent and frightened, he became still more infuriated, and taking her roughly by the arm he pushed her on one side and cried out :

" Yes, you can pass, devil take you, blockhead that you are ! "

VIII

When Kostromsky had quieted down a little after this rude outburst of temper, he at once became weaker, slacker and more drunken than before ; he even forgot that the play had not yet finished. He went into his dressing-room, slowly undressed, and began lazily to rub the paint from his face with vaseline.

The manager, puzzled by his long absence, ran into his room at last and stared in amazement.

" Alexander Yevgrafitch ! Please ! What are you doing ? It's time for you to go on ! "

" Go away, go away ! " muttered Kostromsky

tearfully, speaking through his nose, and wiping his face with the towel. "I've finished everything . . . go away and leave me in peace!"

"What d'you mean, go away? Have you gone out of your mind? The audience is waiting!"

"Leave me alone!" cried Kostromsky.

The manager shrugged his shoulders and went out. In a few moments the curtain was raised, and the public, having been informed of Kostromsky's sudden illness, began to disperse slowly and silently as if they were going away from a funeral.

They had indeed been present at the funeral of a great and original talent, and Kostromsky was right when he said that he had "finished." He had locked the door, and sat by himself in front of the mirror in his dressing-room between two gas burners, the flames of which flared with a slight noise. From old habit he was carefully wiping his face, all smeared over with drunken but bitter tears. His mind recalled, as through a mist, the long line of splendid triumphs which had accompanied the first years of his career. Wreaths . . . bouquets . . . thousands of presents . . . the eternal raptures of the crowd . . . the flattery of newspapers . . . the envy of his companions . . . the fabulous benefits . . . the adoration of the most beautiful of women. . . . Was it possible that all this was past? Could his talent really have gone—vanished? Perhaps it had left him long ago, two or three years back! And he, Kostromsky, what was he now? A theme for dirty theatrical gossip; an object of general mockery and ill-will; a man who had alienated all his friends by his unfeeling narrow-mindedness, his selfishness, his impatience, his unbridled arrogance. . . . Yes, it was all past !

" And if the Almighty "—the well-known lines flashed into his memory—" had not fixed his canon 'gainst self-slaughter. . . . Oh, my God, my God ! " The burning, helpless tears trickled down his erstwhile beautiful face and mingled with the colours of the paint.

All the other actors had left the theatre when Kostromsky came out of his dressing-room. It was almost dark on the stage. Some workmen were wandering about, removing the last decorations. He walked along gropingly, with quiet footfalls, avoiding the heaps of property rubbish which were scattered everywhere about, and making his way towards the street.

Suddenly he was arrested by the sound of the restrained sobbing of a woman.

" Who is there ? " he cried, going into a corner, with an undefined impulse of pity.

The dark figure made no answer ; the sobs increased.

" Who's crying there ? " he asked again, in fear, and at once recognised that it was Yureva who was sobbing there.

The girl was weeping, her thin shoulders heaving with convulsive shudders.

It was strange. For the first time in his life Kostromsky's hard heart suddenly overflowed with a deep pity for this unprotected girl, whom he had so unjustifiably insulted. He placed his hand on her head and began to speak to her in an impressive and affectionate voice, quite naturally and unaffectedly.

" My child ! I was dreadfully rude to you to-day.

I won't ask your forgiveness; I know I could never atone for your tears. But if you could have known what was happening in my soul, perhaps you would forgive me and be sorry for me. . . . To-day, only to-day, I have understood that I have outlived my fame. What grief is there to compare with that? What, in comparison with that, would mean the loss of a mother, of a beloved child, of a lover? We artists live by terrible enjoyments; we live and feel for those hundreds and thousands of people who come to look at us. Do you know . . . oh, you must understand that I'm not showing off, I'm speaking quite simply to you. . . . Yes. Do you know that for the last five years there's not been an actor in the world whose name was greater than mine? Crowds have lain at my feet, at the feet of an illiterate draper's assistant. And suddenly, in one moment, I've fallen headlong from those marvellous heights. . . ." He covered his face with his hands. " It's terrible ! "

Yureva had stopped weeping, and was looking at Kostromsky with deep compassion.

" You see, my dear," he went on, taking her cold hands in his. " You have a great and undoubted talent. Keep on the stage. I won't talk to you about such trivialities as the envy and intrigues of those who cannot act, or about the equivocal protection afforded by patrons of dramatic art, or about the gossip of that marsh which we call Society. All these are trifles, and not to be compared with those stupendous joys which a contemptible but adoring crowd can give to us. But "—Kostromsky's voice trembled nervously—" but do not outlive your fame. Leave the stage directly you feel that the sacred flame in you is burning low. Do not wait, my child, for the public to drive you away."

And turning quickly away from Yureva, who was trying to say something and even holding out her hands to him, he hurriedly walked off the stage.

"Wait a moment, Alexander Yevgrafitch," the manager called after him as he went out into the street, "come into the office for your money."

"Get away!" said Kostromsky, waving his hand, in vexation, irritably. "I have finished. I have finished with it all."

MECHANICAL JUSTICE

THE large hall of the principal club of one of our provincial towns was packed with people. Every box, every seat in pit and stalls was taken, and in spite of the excitement the public was so attentive and quiet that, when the lecturer stopped to take a mouthful of water, everyone could hear a solitary belated fly buzzing at one of the windows.

Amongst the bright dresses of the ladies, white and pink and blue, amongst their bare shoulders and gentle faces shone smart uniforms, dress coats, and golden epaulettes in plenty.

The lecturer, who was clad in the uniform of the Department of Education—a tall man whose yellow face seemed to be made up of a black beard only and glimmering black spectacles—stood at the front of the platform resting his hand on a table.

But the attentive eyes of the audience were directed, not so much on him as on a strange, high, massive-looking contrivance which stood beside him, a grey pyramid covered with canvas, broad at its base, pointed at the top.

Having quenched his thirst, the lecturer went on :

" Let me briefly sum up. What do we see, ladies and gentlemen ? We see that the encouraging system of marks, prizes, distinctions, leads to jealousy, pride and dissatisfaction. Pedagogic suggestion fails at last through repetition. Standing culprits in the corner, on the form, under the clock, making them kneel, is often quite ineffectual as an example, and the victim is sometimes the object of mirth. Shutting in a cell is positively harmful, quite apart from the fact that it uses up the pupil's time without profit. Forced work, on the other hand, robs the work of its true value. Punishment by hunger affects the brain injuriously. The stopping of holidays causes malice in the mind of pupils, and often evokes the dissatisfaction of parents. What remains? Expulsion of the dull or mischievous child from the school—as advised in Holy Writ—the cutting off of the offending member lest, through him, the whole body of the school be infected. Yes, alas! such a measure is, I admit, inevitable on certain occasions now, as inevitable as is capital punishment, I regret to say, even in the best of states. But before resorting to this last irreparable means, let us see what else there may be. . . ."

" And flogging ! " cried a deep bass voice from the front row of the stalls. It was the governor of the town fortress, a deaf old man, under whose chair a pug-dog growled angrily and hoarsely. The governor was a familiar figure about town with his stick, ear trumpet, and old panting pug-dog.

The lecturer bowed, showing his teeth pleasantly.

" I did not intend to express myself as shortly and precisely, but in essence his Excellency has guessed my thought. Yes, ladies and gentlemen, there is one good old Russian method of which we have not yet spoken—corporal punishment. Yes, corporal punishment is part and parcel of the very soul of the great Russian people, of its mighty national sense, its patriotism and deep faith in Providence. Even the apostle said : ' Whom the Lord loveth He chasteneth.' The unforgotten monument of mediæval culture—Domostroi—enjoins the same with paternal firmness. Let us call to mind our inspired Tsar-educator, Peter the Great, with his famous cudgel. Let us call to mind the speech of our immortal Pushkin :

> " ' Our fathers, the further back you go,
> The more the cudgels they used up.'

Finally, let us call to mind our wonderful Gogol, who put into the mouth of a simple, unlearned serving-man the words : ' The peasant must be beaten, for the peasant is being spoiled.' Yes, ladies and gentle-men, I boldly affirm that punishment with rods upon the body goes like a red thread throughout the whole immense course of Russian history, and takes its rise from the very depths of primitive Russian life.

" Thus delving in thought into the past, ladies and gentlemen, I appear a conservative, yet I go forward with outstretched hands to meet the most liberal of humanitarians. I freely allow, loudly confess, that corporal punishment, in the way in which it has been practised until now, has much in it that is insulting for the person being chastised as well as humiliating for the person chastising. The personal confrontment of the two men inevitably awakens hate, fear, irritation, revengefulness, contempt, and what is more, a com-petitive stubbornness in the repetition of crime and punishment. So you no doubt imagine that I renounce corporal punishment. Yes, I do renounce it, though only to introduce it anew, replacing man by a machine.

After the labours, thoughts and experiments of many years, I have at last worked out a scheme of mechanical justice, and have realised it in a machine. Whether I have been successful or not I shall in a minute leave this most respected audience to judge."

The lecturer nodded towards the wings of the stage. A fine-looking attendant came forward and took off the canvas cover from the strange object standing at the footlights. To the eyes of those present, the bright gleaming machine was rather like an automatic weighing-machine, though it was obviously more complex and was much larger. There was a murmur of astonishment among the audience in the hall.

The lecturer extended his hand, and pointed to the apparatus.

"There is my offspring," said he in an agitated voice. "There is an apparatus which may fairly be called the instrument of mechanical justice. The construction is uncommonly simple, and in price it would be within the reach of even a modest village school. Pray consider its construction. In the first place you remark the horizontal platform on springs, and the wooden platform leading to it. On the platform is placed a narrow chair, the back of which has also a powerful spring and is covered with soft leather. Under the chair, as you see, is a system of crescent-shaped levers turning on a hinge. Proportionately with the pressure on the springs of the chair and platform these levers, departing from their equipoise, describe half circles, and close in pairs at a height of from five to eighteen *vershoks* [1] above the level of the chair—varying with the force of pressure.

---

[1] A vershok is $\frac{1}{16}$ of an arshin, *i.e.*, $1\frac{3}{4}$ inches.

Behind the chair rises a vertical cast-iron pillar, with a cross bar. Within the pillar is contained a powerful mechanism resembling that of a watch, having a 160-lb. balance and a spiral spring. On the side of the column observe a little door, that is for cleaning or mending the mechanism. This door has only two keys, and I ask you to note, ladies and gentlemen, that these keys are kept, one by the chief district inspector of mechanical flogging machines, and the other by the head master of the school. So this apparatus, once brought into action, cannot be stopped until it has completed the punishment intended—except, of course, in the eventuality of its being forcibly broken, which is a hardly likely possibility seeing the simplicity and solidity of every part of the machine.

" The watch mechanism, once set going, communicates with a little horizontally-placed axle. The axle has eight sockets in which may be mounted eight long supple bamboo or metal rods. When worn out these can be replaced by new ones. It must be explained also that, by a regulation of the axle, the force of the strokes may be varied.

" And so we see the axle in motion, and moving with it the eight rods. Each rod goes downward perfectly freely, but coming upward again it meets with an obstacle—the cross-beam—and meeting it, bends and is at tension from its point, bulges to a half-circle, and then, breaking free, deals the blow. Then, since the position of the cross-beam can be adjusted, raised or lowered, it will be evident that the tension of the bending rods can be increased or decreased, and the blow given with a greater or less degree of severity. In that way it has been possible to make a scale of severity of punishment from 0 degrees to 24 degrees. No. 0 is when the cross-beam is at its highest point, and is only employed when the punishment bears a merely nominal, or shall I say, symbolical, character. By the time we come to No. 6, a certain amount of pain has become noticeable. We indicate a maximum for use in elementary schools, that would be up to No. 10 ; in secondary schools up to 15. For soldiers, village prisons, and students, the limit is set at 20 degrees, and, finally, for houses of correction and workmen on strike, the maximum figure, namely, 24.

" There, ladies and gentlemen, is the substance of my invention. There remain the details. That handle at the side, like the handle of a barrel organ, serves to wind up the spiral spring of the mechanism. The arrow here in this slot regulates the celerity of the strokes. At the height of the pillar, in a little glass case, is a mechanical meter or indicator. This enables one to check the accuracy of the working of the machine, and is also useful for statistical and revisionary purposes. In view of this latter purpose, the indicator is constructed to show a maximum total of 60,000 strokes. Finally, ladies and gentlemen, please to observe something in the nature of an urn at the foot of the pillar. Into this are thrown metal coupons with numbers on them, and this momentarily sets the whole machine in action. The coupons are of various weights and sizes. The smallest is about the size of a silver penny,[1] and effects the minimum punishment—five strokes. The largest is about the

[1] Five copecks silver—the smallest silver coin in Russia.

size of a hundred-copeck bit—a rouble—and effects a punishment of just one hundred strokes. By using various combinations of metal coupons you can effect a punishment of any number of strokes in a multiple of five, from five to three hundred and fifty. But "—and here the lecturer smiled modestly—" but we should not consider that we had completely solved our problem if it were necessary to stop at that limited figure.

" I will ask you, ladies and gentlemen, to note the figure at which the indicator at present stands, and that which it reaches after the punishment has been effected. What is more, the respected public will observe that, up to the moment when the coupons are thrown into the urn, there is no danger whatever in standing on the platform.

" And so . . . the indicator shows 2900. Consequently, having thrown in all the coupons, the pointer will show, at the end of the execution . . . 3250. . . . I fancy I make no mistake !

" And it will be quite sufficient to throw into the urn anything round, of whatever size, and the machine will go on to infinity, if you will, or, if not to infinity, to 780 or 800, at which point the spring would have run down and the machine need re-winding. What I had in view in using these small coupons was that they might commonly be replaced by coins, and each mechanical self-flogger has a comparative table of the stroke values of copper, silver and gold money. Observe the table here at the side of the main pillar.

" It seems I have finished. . . . There remain just a few particulars concerning the construction of the revolving platform, the swinging chair, and the crescent-shaped levers. But as it is a trifle complicated, I will ask the respected public to watch the machine in action, and I shall now have the honour to give a demonstration.

" The whole procedure of punishment consists in the following. First of all, having thoroughly sifted and got to the bottom of the motives of the crime, we fix the extent of the punishment, that is, the number of strokes, the celerity with which they shall be given, and the force and, in some cases, the material of the rods. Then we send a note to the man in charge of the machine, or communicate with him by telephone. He puts the machine in readiness and then goes away. Observe, the man goes, the machine remains alone, the impartial, unwavering, calm and just machine.

" In a minute I shall come to the experiment. Instead of a human offender we have, on this occasion, a leather mannikin. In order to show the machine at its best we will imagine that we have before us a criminal of the most stubborn type. ' Officer ! ' " cried the lecturer to someone behind the scenes. " ' Prepare the machine, force 24, minimum celerity.' "

In a tense silence the audience watched the attendant wind the handle, push down the cross-beam, turn round the celerity arrow, and then disappear behind the scenes again.

" Now all is in order," the lecturer went on, " and the room in which the flogging machine stands is quite empty. There only remains to call up the man who is to be punished, explain to him the extent of his guilt and the degree of his punishment, and he himself—remark, ladies and gentlemen, himself !— takes from the box the corresponding coupon. Of couɹse, it might be arranged that he, there and then, drops the coupon through a slot in the table and lets it fall into the urn ; that is a mere detail.

" From that moment the offender is entirely in the hands of the machine. He goes to the dressing-room, he opens the door, stands on the platform, throws the coupon or coupons into the urn, and . . . done ! The door shuts mechanically after him, and cannot be re-opened. He may stand a moment, hesitating, on the brink, but in the end he simply must throw the coupons in. For, ladies and gentlemen "— exclaimed the pedagogue with a triumphant laugh— " for the machine is so constructed that the longer he hesitates the greater becomes the punishment, the number of strokes increasing in a ratio of from five to thirty per minute according to the weight of the person hesitating. . . . However, once the offender is off, he is caught by the machine at three points, neck, waist and feet, and the chair holds him. All this is accomplished literally in one moment. The next moment sounds the first stroke, and nothing can stop the action of the machine, nor weaken the blows, nor increase or diminish the celerity, until that moment when justice has been accomplished. It would be physically impossible, not having the key.

" Officer ! Bring in the mannikin !

" Will the esteemed audience kindly indicate the number of the strokes. . . . Just a number, please . . . three figures if you wish, but not more than 350. Please. . . ."

" Five hundred," shouted the governor of the fortress.

" Reff," barked the dog under his chair.

" Five hundred is too many," gently objected the lecturer, " but to go as far as we can towards meeting his Excellency's wish let us say 350. We throw into the urn all the coupons."

Whilst he was speaking, the attendant brought in under his arm a monstrous-looking leathern mannikin, and stood it on the floor, holding it up from behind. There was something suggestive and ridiculous in the crooked legs, outstretched arms, and forward-hanging head of this leathern dummy.

Standing on the platform of the machine, the lecturer continued :

" Ladies and gentlemen, one last word. I do not doubt that my mechanical self-flogger will be most widely used. Slowly but surely it will find its way into all schools, colleges and seminaries. It will be introduced in the army and navy, in the village, in military and civil prisons, in police stations and for fire-brigades, and in all truly Russian families.

" The coupons are inevitably replaced by coins, and in that way not only is the cost of the machine redeemed, but a fund is commenced which can be used for charitable and educative ends. Our eternal financial troubles will pass, for, by the aid of this machine, the peasant will be forced to pay his taxes. Sin will disappear, crime, laziness, slovenliness, and in their stead will flourish industry, temperance, sobriety and thrift.

" It is difficult to probe further the possible future of this machine. Did Gutenberg foresee the contribution which book-printing was going to make to the history of human progress when he made his first naïve wooden printing-press ? But I am, however, far from airing a foolish self-conceit in your eyes, ladies and gentlemen. The bare idea belongs to me. In the practical details of the invention I have received most material help from Mr. N——, the teacher of physics in the Fourth Secondary School of this town, and from Mr. X——, the well-known engineer. I take the opportunity of acknowledging my indebtedness."

The hall thundered with applause. Two men in the front of the stalls stood up timidly and awkwardly, and bowed to the public.

"For me personally," continued the lecturer, "there has been the greatest satisfaction to consider the good I was doing my beloved fatherland. Here, ladies and gentlemen, is a token which I have lately received from the governor and nobility of Kursk — with the motto : *Similia similibus*."

He detached from its chain and held aloft an immense antique chronometer, about half a pound in weight. From the watch dangled also a massive gold medal.

"I have finished, ladies and gentlemen," added the lecturer in a low and solemn voice, bowing as he spoke.

But the applause had not died down before there happened something incredible, appalling. The chronometer suddenly slipped from the raised hand of the pedagogue, and fell with a metallic clash right into the urn.

At once the machine began to hum and click. The platform inverted, and the lecturer was suddenly hoist with his own petard. His coat-tails waved in the air ; there was a sudden thwack and a wild cry.

2901, indicated the mechanical reckoner.

It is difficult to describe rapidly and definitely what happened in the meeting. For a few seconds everyone was turned to stone. In the general silence sounded only the cries of the victim, the whistling of the rods, and the clicking of the counting machine. Then suddenly everyone rushed up on to the stage.

" For the love of the Lord ! " cried the unfortunate man, " for the love of the Lord ! "

But it was impossible to help him. The valorous physics teacher put out a hand to catch one of the rods as they came, but drew it back at once, and the blood on his fingers was visible to all. No efforts could raise the cross-beam.

" The key ! Quick, the key ! " cried the pedagogue. " In my trouser pocket."

The devoted attendant dashed in to search his pockets, with difficulty avoiding blows from the machine. But the key was not to be found.

2950, 2951, 2952, 2953, clicked the counting machine.

" Oh, your honour ! " cried the attendant through his tears. " Let me take your trousers off. They are quite new, and they will be ruined. . . . Ladies can turn the other way."

" Go to blazes, idiot ! Oey, o, o ! . . . Gentlemen, for God's sake ! . . . Oey, oey ! . . . I forgot. . . . The keys are in my overcoat. . . . Oey ! Quickly ! "

They ran to the ante-room for his overcoat. But neither was there any key there. Evidently the inventor had left it at home. Someone was sent to fetch it. A gentleman present offered his carriage.

And the sharp blows registered themselves every second with mathematical precision ; the pedagogue shouted ; the counting machine went indifferently on.

3180, 3181, 3182. . . .

One of the garrison lieutenants drew his sword and began to hack at the apparatus, but after the fifth blow there remained only the hilt, and a jumping splinter hit the president of the Zemstvo. Most dreadful of all was the fact that it was impossible to guess to what point the flogging would go on. The chronometer was proving itself weighty. The man sent for the key still did not return, and the counter, having long since passed the figure previously indicated by the inventor, went on placidly.

3999, 4000, 4001.

The pedagogue jumped no longer. He just lay with gaping mouth and protruding eyes, and only twitched convulsively.

At last, the governor of the fortress, boiling with indignation, roared out to the accompaniment of the barking of his dog :

" Madness ! Debauch ! Unheard of ! Order up the fire-brigade ! "

This idea was the wisest. The governor of the town was an enthusiast for the fire-brigade, and had smartened the firemen to a rare pitch. In less than five minutes, and at that moment when the indicator showed stroke No. 4550, the brave young fellows of the fire-brigade broke on the scene with choppers and hooks.

The magnificent mechanical self-flogger was destroyed for ever and ever. With the machine perished also the idea. As regards the inventor, it should be said that, after a considerable time of feeling sore in a corporal way and of nervous weakness, he returned to his occupation. But the fatal occasion completely changed his character. He became for the rest of his life a calm, sweet, melancholy man, and though he taught Latin and Greek he was a favourite with the schoolboys.

He has never returned to his invention.

VIII

THE LAST WORD

YES, gentlemen, I killed him !

In vain do you try to obtain for me a medical certificate of temporary aberration. I shall not take advantage of it.

I killed him soberly, conscientiously, coldly, without the least regret, fear or hesitation. Were it in your power to resurrect him, I would repeat my crime.

He followed me always and everywhere. He took a thousand human shapes, and did not shrink—shameless creature—to dress in women's clothes upon occasion. He took the guise of my relative, my dear friend, colleague, good acquaintance. He could dress to look any age except that of a child (as a child he only failed and looked ridiculous). He has filled up my life with himself, and poisoned it.

What has been most dreadful was that I have always foreseen in advance all his words, gestures and actions.

When I met him he would drawl, crushing my hand in his :

" Aha ! Whom—do—I—see ? Dear me ! You must be getting on in years now. How's your health ? "

Then he would answer as for himself, though I had not asked him anything :

" Thank you. So so. Nothing to boast of. Have you read in to-day's paper . . . ? "

If he by any chance noticed that I had a flushed cheek, flushed by the vexation of having met him, he would be sure to croak :

" Eh, neighbour, how red you're getting."

He would come to me just at those moments when I was up to the neck in work, would sit down and say :

" Ah ! I'm afraid I've interrupted you."

For two hours he would bore me to death, prattling of himself and his children. He would see I was tearing my hair and biting my lips till the blood came, and would simply delight in my torments.

Having poisoned my working mood for a whole month in advance, he would stand, yawn a little, and then murmur :

" Lord knows why I stay here talking. I've got lots to do."

When I met him in a railway carriage he always began :

" Permit me to ask, are you going far ? " And then :

" On business or . . . ? "

" Where do you work ? "

" Married ? "

Oh, well do I know all his ways. Closing my eyes I see him. He strikes me on the shoulder, on the back, on the knees. He gesticulates so closely to my eyes and nose that I wince, as if about to be struck. Catching hold of the lappet of my coat, he draws himself up to me and breathes in my face. When he visits me he allows his foot to tremble on the floor under the table, so that the shade of the lamp tinkles.

At an " at home " he thrums on the back of my chair with his fingers, and in pauses of the conversation drawls, " y-e-s, y-es." At cards he calls out, knocks on the table and quacks as he loses : " What's that ? What ?   What ? "

Start him in an argument, and he always begins by :

" Eh, neighbour, it's humbug you're talking."

" Why humbug ? " you ask timidly.

" Because it is nonsense."

What evil have I done to this man ?   I don't know. He set himself to spoil my existence, and he spoiled it.   Thanks to him, I now feel a great aversion from the sea, the moon, the air, poetry, painting, music.

" Tolstoy "—he bawled orally, and in print — " made his estate over to his wife, and he himself. . . . Compared with Turgenief, he. . . . He sewed his own jack-boots . . . great writer of the Russian earth. . . . Hurrah ! . . .

" Pushkin ?   He created the language, didn't he ? Do you remember ' Calm was the Ukraine night, clear was the sky ' ?   You remember what they did to the woman in the third act.   Hsh !   There are no ladies present, do you remember ?

"' In our little boat we go,
Under the little boat the water.'

" Dostoevsky . . . have you read how he went one night to Turgenief to confess . . . Gogol, do you know the sort of disease he had ? "

Should I go to a picture gallery, and stand before some quiet evening landscape, he would be sure to be on my heels, pushing me forward, and saying to a girl on his arm :

" Very   sweetly   drawn . . . distance . . . atmosphere . . . the moon to the life. . . . Do you remember Nina—the coloured supplement of the *Neva* [1]—it was something like it. . . ."

I sit at the opera listening t ɔ " Carmen." He is there, as everywhere. He is behind me, and has his feet on the lower bar of my fauteuil. He hums the tune of the duet in the last act, and through his feet communicates to my nerves every movement of his body. Then, in the entr'act, I hear him speaking in a voice pitched high enough for me to hear :

" Wonderful gramophone records the Zadodadofs have. Shalapin absolutely. You couldn't tell the difference."

Yes, it was he or someone like him who invented the barrel organ, the gramophone, the bioscope, the photophone, the biograph, the phonograph, the pathephone, the musical box, the pianino, the motor car, paper collars, oleographs, and newspapers.

There's no getting away from him. I flee away at night to the wild seashore, and lie down in solitude upon a cliff, but he steals after me in the shadow, and suddenly the silence is broken by a self-satisfied voice which says :

" What a lovely night, Katenka, isn't it ? The clouds, eh, look at them ! Just as in a picture. And if a painter painted them just like it, who would say it was true to Natuɪe ? "

He has killed the best minutes of my life—minutes of love, the dear sweet nights of youth. How often, when I have wandered arm in arm with the most beauteous cɪeation of Nature, along an avenue where, upon the ground, the silver moonlight was in pattern

---

[1] A popular Russian journal.

with the shadows of the trees, and he has suddenly and unexpectedly spoken up to me in a woman's voice, has rested his head on my shoulder and cried out in a theatrical tone :

" Tell me, do you love to dream by moonlight ? "

Or :

" Tell me, do you love Nature ? As for me, I madly adore Nature."

He was many shaped and many faced, my persecutor, but was always the same underneath. He took upon occasion the guise of professor, doctor, engineer, lady doctor, advocate, girl-student, author, wife of the excise inspector, official, passenger, customer, guest, stranger, spectator, reader, neighbour at a country house. In early youth I had the stupidity to think that these were all separate people. But they were all one and the same. Bitter experience has at last discovered to me his name. It is—the Russian *intelligent*.

If he has at any time missed me personally, he has left everywhere his traces, his visiting cards. On the heights of Barchau and Machuka I have found his orange peelings, sardine tins, and chocolate wrappings. On the rocks of Aloopka, on the top of the belfry of St. John, on the granites of Imatra, on the walls of Bakhchisari, in the grotto of Lermontof, I have found the following signatures and remarks :—

" Pusia and Kuziki 1908 year 27 February."

" Ivanof."

" A. M. Plokhokhostof (Bad-tail) from Saratof."

" Ivanof."

" Pechora girl."

" Ivanof."

"M.D. . . . P.A.P. . . . Talotchka and Achmet."
" Ivanof."
"Trophim Sinepupof.   Samara Town."
" Ivanof."
" Adel Soloveitchik from Minsk."
" Ivanof."
" From this height I delighted in the view of the
sea.—C. NICODEMUS IVANOVITCH BEZUPRECHNY."
" Ivanof."

I have read his verses and remarks in all visiting
books, and in Puskhin's house, at Lermontof's Cliff,
and in the ancient monasteries have read : " The
Troakofs came here from Penza, drank kvas and ate
sturgeon.   We wish the same to you," or " Visited
the natal ash-tray of the great Russian poet, Chichkin,
teacher of caligraphy, Voronezh High School for
Boys," or—

> " Praise to thee, Ai Petri, mountain white,
>   In dress imperial of fir.
> I climbed up yesterday unto thy height,
>   Retired Staff-Captain Nikoli Profer."

I needed but to pick up my favourite Russian book,
and I came upon him at once.   " I have read this
book.—PAFNUTENKO."   " The author is a blockhead."
" Mr. Author hasn't read Karl Marx."   I turn over
the pages, and I find his notes in all the margins.
Then, of course, no one like he turns down corners
and makes dog-ears, tears out pages, or drops grease
on them from tallow candles.

Gentlemen, judges, it is hard for me to go on.
This man has abused, fouled, vulgarised all that was
dear to me, delicate and touching.   I struggled a
long while with myself.   Years went by.   My nerves

became more irritable. I saw there was not room for both of us in the world. One of us had to go.

I foresaw for a long while that it would be just some little trifle that would drive me to the crime. So it was.

You know the particulars. In the compartment there was a crush; the passengers were sitting on one another's heads. He, with his wife, his son, a schoolboy in the preparatory class, and a pile of luggage, were occupying four seats. Upon this occasion he was wearing the uniform of the Department of Popular Education. I went up to him and asked:

" Is there not a free seat here ? "

He answered like a bulldog with a bone, not looking at me:

" No. This seat is taken by another gentleman. These are his things. He'll be back in a minute."

The train began to move.

I waited, standing, where I was. We went on about ten miles. The gentleman didn't come. I was silent, and I looked into the face of the pedagogue, thinking that there might yet be in him some gleam of conscience.

But no. We went another fifteen miles. He got down a basket of provisions and began to eat. He went out with a kettle for hot water, and made himself tea. A little domestic scandal arose over the sugar for the tea.

" Peter, you've taken a lump of sugar on the sly ! "

" Word of honour, by God, I haven't ! Look in my pockets, by God ! "

" Don't swear, and don't lie. I counted them before we set out, on purpose. . . . There were eighteen and now there are seventeen."

" By God ! ! "

" Don't swear. It is shameful to lie. I will forgive you everything, only tell me straight out the truth. But a lie I can never forgive. Only cowards lie. One who is capable of lying is capable of murdering, of stealing, of betraying his king and his country. . . ."

So he ran on and ran on. I had heard such utterances from him in my earliest childhood, when he was my governess, afterwards when he was my class teacher, and again when he wrote in the newspaper.

I interrupted.

" You find fault with your son for lying, and yet you yourself have, in his presence, told a whopping lie. You said this seat was occupied by a gentleman. Where is that gentleman ? Show him to me."

The pedagogue went purple, and his eyes dilated.

"I beg you, don't interfere with people who don't interfere with you. Mind your own business. How scandalous ! Conductor, please warn this passenger that he will not be allowed to interfere with other people in the railway carriage. Please take measures, or I'll report the matter to the gendarme, and write in the complaint book."

The conductor screwed up his eyes in a fatherly expression, and went out. But the pedagogue went on, unconsoled :

" No one speaks to you. No one was interfering with you. Good Lord ! a decent-looking man too, in a hat and a collar, clearly one of the *intelligentia*. . . . A peasant now, or a workman . . . but no, an intelligent ! "

Intel-li-gent ! The executioner had named me executioner ! It was ended. . . . He had pronounced his own sentence.

I took out of the pocket of my overcoat a revolver, examined the charge, pointed it at the pedagogue between the eyes, and said calmly :

" Say your prayers."

He turned pale and shrieked :

" Guard-d-d ! . . ."

That was his last word. I pulled the trigger.

I have finished, gentlemen. I repeat : I do not repent. There is no sorrow for him in my soul. One desolating doubt remains, however, and it will haunt me to the end of my days, should I finish them in prison or in an asylum.

He has a son left ! What if he takes on his father's nature ?

IX

THE WHITE POODLE

I

By narrow mountain paths, from one villa to another, a small wandering troupe made their way along the southern shore of the Crimea. Ahead commonly ran the white poodle, Arto, with his long red tongue hanging out from one side of his mouth. The pcodle was shorn to look like a lion. At crossways he would stop, wag his tail, and look back questioningly. He seemed to obtain some sort of sign, known to him alone, and without waiting for the troupe to catch up he would bound forward on the right track, shaking his shaggy ears, never making a mistake. Following the dog came the twelve-year-old Sergey, carrying under his left arm a little mattress for his acrobatic exercises, and holding in his right hand a narrow dirty cage, with a goldfinch, taught to pull out from a case various coloured papers on which were printed predictions of coming fortune. Last of all came the oldest member of the troupe, grandfather Martin Lodishkin, with a barrel organ on his bent back.

The organ was an old one, very hoarse, and suffering from a cough ; it had undergone, in the century of its existence, some scores of mendings. It played two things : a melancholy German waltz of Launer and a galop from " A Trip to China Town," both in fashion thirty to forty years ago, but now forgotten by all.   Beyond these drawbacks it must be said that the organ had two false tubes ; one of them, a treble, was absolutely mute, did not play, and therefore when its turn came the whole harmony would, as it were, stutter, go lame and stumble.   The other tube, giving forth a bass note, had something the matter with the valve, which would not shut, and having once been played it would not altogether stop, but rolled onward on the same bass note, deafening and confusing the other sounds, till suddenly, at its own caprice, it would stop.   Grandfather himself acknowledged the deficiencies of his instrument, and might sometimes be heard to remark jocosely, though with a tinge of secret grief :

" What's to be done ? . . . An ancient organ . . . it has a cold. . . . When you play it the gentry take offence.   ' Tfu,' they say, ' what a wretched thing ! ' And these pieces were very good in their time, and fashionable, but people nowadays by no means adore good music.   Give them ' The Geisha,' ' Under the Double-headed Eagle,' please, or the waltz from ' The Seller of Birds.'   Of course, these tubes. . . . I took the organ to the shop, but they wouldn't undertake to mend it.   ' It needs new tubes,' said they. ' But, best of all, if you'll take our advice, sell the rusty thing to a museum . . . as a sort of curio. . . .'   Well, well, that's enough !   She's fed us till now, Sergey and me, and if God grant, she will go on feeding us."

Grandfather Martin Lodishkin loved his organ as it is only possible to love something living, near, something actually akin, if it may be so expressed,

Having lived with his organ for many years of a trying vagabond life, he had at last come to see in it something inspired, come to feel as if it were almost a conscious being. It would happen sometimes at night, when they were lying on the floor of some dirty inn, that the barrel organ, placed beside the old man's pillow, would suddenly give vent to a faint note, a sad melancholy quavering note, like an old man's sigh. And Lodishkin would put out his hand to its carved wooden side and whisper caressingly :

" What is it, brother ? Complaining, eh ! . . . Have patience, friend. . . ."

And as much as Lodishkin loved his organ, and perhaps even a little more, he loved the other two companions of his wanderings, Arto, the poodle, and little Sergey. He had hired the boy five years before from a bad character, a widower cobbler, promising to pay him two roubles a month. Shortly afterwards the cobbler had died, and Sergey remained with grandfather, bound to him for ever by their common life and the little daily interests of the troupe.

II

The path went along a high cliff over the sea, and wandered through the shade of ancient olive trees. The sea gleamed between the trunks now and then, and seemed at times to stand like a calm and mighty wall on the horizon ; its colour was the more blue, the more intense, because of the contrast seen through the trellis-work of silver verdant leaves. In the grass, amongst the kizil shrubs, wild roses and vines, and even on the branches of the trees, swarmed the grasshoppers, and the air itself trembled from the

monotonously sounding and unceasing murmur of
their legs and wing-cases. The day turned out to be
a sultry one ; there was no wind, and the hot earth
burnt the soles of the feet.

Sergey, going as usual ahead of grandfather, stopped,
and waited for the old man to catch up to him.

" What is it, Serozha ? " asked the organ-grinder.

" The heat, grandfather Lodishkin . . . there's no
bearing it ! To bathe would be good. . . ."

The old man wiped his perspiring face with his
sleeve, and hitched the organ to a more comfortable
position on his back.

" What would be better ? " he sighed, looking
eagerly downward to the cool blueness of the sea.
" Only, after bathing, one gets more hungry, you
know. A village doctor once said to me : ' Salt has
more effect on man than anything else . . . that
means, it weakens him . . . sea-salt. . . .' "

" He lied, perhaps," remarked Sergey, doubtfully.

" Lied ! What next ? Why should he lie ? A
solid man, non-drinker . . . having a little house in
Sevastopol. What's more, there's no getting down
to the sea here. Wait a bit, we'll get to Miskhor,
and there rinse our sinful bodies. It's fine to bathe
before dinner . . . and afterwards to sleep, we three
. . . and a splendid bit of work. . . ."

Arto, hearing conversation behind him, turned and
ran back, his soft blue eyes, half shut from the heat,
looked up appealingly, and his hanging tongue trembled
from quick breathing.

" What is it, brother doggie ? Warm, eh ? "
asked grandfather.

The dog yawned, straining his jaws and curling

his tongue into a little tube, shook all his body, and whimpered.

" Yes, yes, little brother, but it can't be helped," continued Lodishkin. " It is written, ' In the sweat of thy face,' though, as a matter of fact, it can hardly be said that you have a face, or anything more than a muzzle. . . . Be off ! Go off with you. . . . As for me, Serozha, I must confess I just like this heat. Only the organ's a bit of a nuisance, and if there were no work to do I'd just lie down somewhere in the grass in the shade, and have a good morning of it. For old bones this sunshine is the finest thing in the world."

The footpath turned downward to a great highway, broad and hard and blindingly white. At the point where the troupe stepped on to it commenced an ancient baronial estate, in the abundant verdure of which were beautiful villas, flower-beds, orangeries and fountains. Lodishkin knew the district well, and called at each of the villas every year, one after another, during the vine-harvesting season, when the whole Crimea is filled with rich, fashionable, and pleasure-loving visitors. The bright magnificence of southern Nature did not touch the old man, but it enraptured Sergey, who was there for the first time. The magnolias, with their hard and shiny leaves, shiny as if lacquered or varnished, with their large white blossoms, each almost as big as a dinner-plate ; the summer-houses of interwoven vines hanging with heavy clusters of fruit ; the enormous century-old plane trees, with their bright trunks and mighty crowns ; tobacco plantations, rivulets, waterfalls, and everywhere, in flower-beds, gardens, on the walls of the villas, bright sweet-scented roses—all these things impressed unceasingly the naïve soul of the boy. He expressed his admiration of the scene, pulling the old man's sleeve and crying out every minute :

"Grandfather Lodishkin, but, grandfather, just look, goldfish in the fountain ! . . . I swear, grandfather, goldfish, if I die for it ! " cried the boy, pressing his face to a railing and staring at a large tank in the middle of a garden. " I say, grandfather, look at the peaches ! Good gracious, what a lot there are. Look, how many ! And all on one tree."

" Leave go, leave go, little stupid. What are you stretching your mouth about ? " joked the old man. " Just wait till we get to the town of Novorossisk, and give ourselves to the South. Now, that's a place indeed ; there you'll see something. Sotchi, Adler, Tuapse, and then, little brother, Sukhum, Batum. . . . Your eyes'll drop out of your head. . . . Palms, for instance. Absolutely astonishing ; the trunks all shaggy like felt, and each leaf so large that we could hide ourselves in one."

" You don't mean it ! " cried Sergey, joyfully.

" Wait a bit and you'll see for yourself. Is there little of anything there ? Now, oranges for instance, or, let us say, lemons. . . . You've seen them, no doubt, in the shops ? "

" Well ? "

" Well, you see them simply as if they were growing in the air. Without anything, just on the tree, as up here you see an apple or a pear. . . . And the people down there, little brother, are altogether out of the way : Turks, Persians, different sorts of Cherkesses, and all in gowns and with daggers, a desperate sort of

people ! And, little brother, there are even Ethiopians.
I've seen them many times in Batum ! ''

" Ethiopians, I know. Those with horns," cried
Sergey, confidently.

" Well, horns I suppose they have not," said grandfather ; " that's nonsense. But they're black as a
pair of boots, and shine even. Thick, red, ugly lips,
great white eyes, and hair as curly as the back of a
black sheep."

" Oi, oi, how terrible ! . . . Are Ethiopians like
that ? ''

" Well, well, don't be frightened. Of course, at
first, before you're accustomed, it's alarming. But
when you see that other people aren't afraid, you
pick up courage. . . . There's all sorts there, little
brother. When we get there you'll see. Only one
thing is bad—the fever. All around lie marshes,
rottenness ; then there is such terrible heat. The
people who live there find it all right, but it's bad for
new-comers. However, we've done enough tongue-
wagging, you and I, Sergey, so just climb over
that stile and go up to the house. There are
some really fine people living there. . . . If ever
there's anything you want to know, just ask me ; I
know all."

But the day turned out to be a very unsuccessful
one for them. At one place the servants drove them
away almost before they were seen even from a distance
by the mistress ; at another the organ had hardly
made its melancholy beginning in front of the balcony
when they were waved away in disgust ; at a third
they were told that the master and mistress had not
yet arrived. At two villas they were indeed paid

for their show, but very little. Still, grandfather never turned his nose up even at the smallest amounts. Coming out at the gate on to the road he would smile good-naturedly and say :

" Two plus five, total seven . . . hey hey, brother Serozhenka, that's money. Seven times seven, and you've pretty well got a shilling, and that would be a good meal and a night's lodging in our pockets, and p'raps, old man Lodishkin might be allowed a little glass on account of his weakness. . . . Ai, ai, there's a sort of people I can't make out ; too stingy to give sixpence, yet ashamed to put in a penny . . . and so they surlily order you off. Better to give, were it only three farthings. . . . I wouldn't take offence, I'm nobody . . . why take offence ? "

Generally speaking, Lodishkin was of a modest order, and even when he was hounded out of a place he would not complain. However, on this day of which we are writing, he was, as it happened, disturbed out of his usual equanimity by one of the people of these Crimean villas, a lady of a very kind appearance, the owner of a beautiful country house surrounded by a wonderful flower-garden. She listened attentively to the music ; watched Sergey's somersaults and Arto's tricks even more attentively ; asked the little boy's age, what was his name, where he'd learned gymnastics, how grandfather had come by him, what his father had done for a living, and so on, and had then bidden them wait, and had gone indoors apparently to fetch them something.

Ten minutes passed, a quarter of an hour, and she did not appear, but the longer she stayed the greater became the vague hopes of the troupe. Grandfather even whispered to Sergey, shielding his mouth with his palm the while :

" Eh, Sergey, this is good, isn't it ? Ask me if you want to know anything. Now we're going to get some old clothes or perhaps a pair of boots. A sure thing ! . . ."

At last the lady came out on her balcony again, and flung into Sergey's held-out hat a small silver coin. And then she went in again. The coin turned out to be an old worn-out threepenny bit with a hole in it. No use to buy anything with. Grandfather held it in his hand and considered it a long while distrustfully. He left the house and went back to the road, and all the while he still held the bit of money in his open and extended palm, as if weighing it as he went.

" Well, well. . . . That's smart ! " said he at last, stopping suddenly. " I must say. . . . And didn't we three blockheads do our best. It'd a-been better if she'd given us a button. That, at least, we could have sewn on somewhere. What's the use of this bit of rubbish ? The lady, no doubt, thought that it would be all the same as a good coin to me. I'd pass it off on someone at night. No, no, you're deeply mistaken, my lady. Old man Lodishkin is not going to descend so low. Yes, m'lady, there goes your precious threepenny bit ! There ! "

And with indignation and pride he flung the coin on to the road, and it gently jingled and was lost in the dust.

So the morning passed, and the old man and the boy, having passed all the villas on the cliff, prepared to go down to the sea. There remained but one last estate on the way. This was on the left-hand side.

The house itself was not visible, the wall being high, and over the wall loomed a fine array of dusty cypresses. Only through the wide cast-iron gate, whose fantastical design gave it the appearance of lace, was it possible to get a glimpse of the lovely lawn. Thence one peered upon fresh green grass, flower-beds, and in the background a winding pergola of vines. In the middle of the lawn stood a gardener watering the roses. He put a finger to the pipe in his hand, and caused the water in the fountain to leap in the sun, glittering in myriads of little sparkles and flashes.

Grandfather was going past, but looking through the gate he stopped in doubt.

" Wait a bit, Sergey," said he. " Surely there are no folk here! There's a strange thing! Often as I've come along this road, I've never seen a soul here before. Oh, well, brother Sergey, get ready!"

A notice was fixed on the wall:

" Friendship Villa : Trespassers will be prosecuted," and Sergey read this out aloud.

" Friendship ? " questioned grandfather, who himself could not read. " Vo-vo! That's one of the finest of words—friendship. All day we've failed, but this house will make up for it. I smell it with my nose, as if I were a hunting dog. Now, Arto, come here, old fellow. Walk up bravely, Serozha. Keep your eye on me, and if you want to know anything just ask me. I know all."

III

The paths were made of a well-rolled yellow gravel, crunching under the feet ; and at the sides were borders of large rose - coloured shells. In the flower - beds, above a carpet of various coloured grasses, grew rare plants with brilliant blossoms and sweet perfume. Crystal water rose and splashed continually from the fountains, and garlands of beautiful creeping plants hung downward from beautiful vases, suspended in mid-air from wires stretched between the trees. On marble pillars just outside the house stood two splendid spheres of mirror glass, and the wandering troupe, coming up to them, saw themselves reflected feet upwards in an amusing twisted and elongated picture.

In front of the balcony was a wide, much-trampled platform. On this Sergey spread his little mattress, and grandfather, having fixed the organ on its stick, prepared to turn the handle. But just as he was in the act of doing this, a most unexpected and strange sight suddenly attracted his attention.

A boy of nine or ten rushed suddenly out of the house on to the terrace like a bomb, giving forth piercing shrieks. He was in a sailor suit, with bare arms and legs. His fair curls hung in a tangle on his shoulders. Away he rushed, and after him came six people ; two women in aprons, a stout old lackey, without moustache or beard but with grey side-whiskers, wearing a frock coat, a lean, carrotty-haired, red-nosed girl in a blue-checked dress, a young sickly-looking but very beautiful lady in a blue dressing-jacket trimmed with lace, and, last of all, a stout, bald gentleman in a suit of Tussore silk, and with gold spectacles. They were all very much excited, waved their arms, spoke loudly, and even jostled one another. You could see at once that the cause of all their anxiety was the boy in the sailor suit, who had so suddenly rushed on to the terrace.

And the boy, the cause of all this hurly-burly, did not cease screaming for one second, but threw himself down on his stomach, turned quickly over on to his back, and began to kick out with his legs on all sides. The little crowd of grown-ups fussed around him. The old lackey in the frock coat pressed his hands to his starched shirt - front and begged and implored the boy to be quiet, his long side-whiskers trembling as he spoke :

" Little father, master ! . . . Nikolai Apollonovitch ! . . . Do not vex your little mamma. Do get up, sir ; be so good, so kind—take a little, sir. The mixture's sweet as sweet, just syrup, sir. Now let me help you up. . . ."

The women in the aprons clapped their hands and chirped quickly-quickly, in seemingly passionate and frightened voices. The red-nosed girl made tragic gestures, and cried out something evidently very touching, but completely incomprehensible, as it was in a foreign language. The gentleman in the gold spectacles made speeches to the boy in a reasoning bass voice, wagged his head to and fro as he spoke, and slowly waved his hands up and down. And the beautiful, delicate - looking lady moaned wearily, pressing a lace handkerchief to her eyes.

" Ah, Trilly, ah, God in Heaven ! . . . Angel mine, I beseech you, listen, your own mother begs you. Now do, do take the medicine, take it and you'll see, you'll feel better at once, and the stomach-ache will go away and the headache. Now do it for me, my joy ! Oh, Trilly, if you want it, your mamma will go down on her knees. See, darling, I'm on my knees before you. If you wish it, I'll give you gold—a sovereign, two sovereigns, five sovereigns. Trilly, would you like a live ass ? Would you like a live horse ? Oh, for goodness' sake, say something to him, doctor."

" Pay attention, Trilly. Be a man ! " droned the stout gentleman in the spectacles.

" Ai-yai-yai-ya-a-a-a ! " yelled the boy, squirming on the ground, and kicking about desperately with his feet.

Despite his extreme agitation he managed to give several kicks to the people around him, and they, for their part, got out of his way sufficiently cleverly.

Sergey looked upon the scene with curiosity and astonishment, and at last nudged the old man in the side and said :

" Grandfather Lodishkin, what's the matter with him ? Can't they give him a beating ? "

" A beating—I like that. . . . That sort isn't beaten, but beats everybody else. A crazy boy ; ill, I expect."

" Insane ? " enquired Sergey.

" How should I know ? Hst, be quiet ! . . ."

" Ai-yai-ya-a ! Scum, fatheads ! " shouted the boy, louder and louder.

" Well, begin, Sergey. Now's the time, for I know ! " ordered Lodishkin suddenly, taking hold of the handle of his organ and turning it with resolution. The snuffling and false notes of the ancient galop rose in the garden. All the people stopped suddenly and looked round ; even the boy became silent for a few seconds.

" Ah, God in heaven, they will upset my poor
Trilly still more ! " cried the lady in the blue dressing-
jacket, with tears in her eyes. Chase them off, quickly,
quickly. Drive them away, and the dirty dog with
them. Dogs have always such dreadful diseases.
Why do you stand there helplessly, Ivan, as if you
were turned to stone ? She shook her handkerchief
wearily in the direction of grandfather and the little
boy ; the lean, red-nosed girl made dreadful eyes ;
someone gave a threatening whisper ; the lackey
in the dress coat ran swiftly from the balcony on his
tiptoes, and, with an expression of horror on his face,
cried to the organ grinder, spreading out his arms like
wings as he spoke :

" Whatever does it mean—who permitted them—
who let them through ? March ! Clear out ! . . . "

The organ became silent in a melancholy whimper.

" Fine gentleman, allow us to explain," began the
old man delicately.

" No explanations whatever ! March ! " roared the
lackey in a hoarse, angry whisper.

His whole fat face turned purple, and his eyes
protruded to such a degree that they looked as if they
would suddenly roll out and run away like wheels.
The sight was so dreadful that grandfather involuntarily took two steps backward.

" Put the things up, Sergey," said he, hurriedly
jolting the organ on to his back. " Come on ! "

But they had not succeeded in taking more than
ten steps when the child began to shriek even worse
than ever :

" Ai-yai-yai ! Give it me ! I wa-ant it ! A-a-a !
Give it ! Call them back ! Me ! "

" But, Trilly ! . . . Ah, God in heaven, Trilly ; ah, call them back ! " moaned the nervous lady. " Tfu, how stupid you all are ! . . . Ivan, don't you hear when you're told ? Go at once and call those beggars back ! . . ."

" Certainly ! You ! Hey, what d'you call your-selves ? Organ grinders ! Come back ! " cried several voices at once.

The stout lackey jumped across the lawn, his side-whiskers waving in the wind, and, overtaking the artistes, cried out :

" Pst ! Musicians ! Back ! Don't you hear, friends, you're called back ? " cried he, panting and waving both arms. " Venerable old man ! " said he at last, catching hold of grandfather's coat by the sleeve. " Turn the shafts round. The master and mistress will be pleased to see your pantomime."

" Well, well, business at last ! " sighed grandfather, turning his head round. And the little party went back to the balcony where the people were collected, and the old man fixed up his organ on the stick and played the hideous galop from the very point at which it had been interrupted.

The rumpus had died down. The lady with her little boy, and the gentleman in the gold spectacles, came forward. The others remained respectfully behind. Out of the depths of the shrubbery came the gardener in his apron, and stood at a little distance. From somewhere or other the yard-porter made his appearance, and stood behind the gardener. He was an immense bearded peasant with a gloomy face, narrow brows, and pock-marked cheeks. He was clad in a new rose-

coloured blouse, on which was a pattern of large
black spots.

Under cover of the hoarse music of the galop,
Sergey spread his little mattress, pulled off his canvas
breeches—they had been cut out of an old sack,
and behind, at the broadest part, were ornamented
by a quadrilateral trade mark of a factory—threw
from his body his torn shirt, and stood erect in his
cotton underclothes. In spite of the many mends
on these garments he was a pretty figure of a boy,
lithe and strong. He had a little programme of
acrobatic tricks which he had learnt by watching
his elders in the arena of the circus. Running to the
mattress he would put both hands to his lips, and,
with a passionate gesture, wave two theatrical kisses
to the audience. So his performance began.

Grandfather turned the handle of the organ without
ceasing, and whilst the boy juggled various objects
in the air the old music-machine gave forth its trembling,
coughing tunes. Sergey's repertoire was not a large
one, but he did it well and with enthusiasm. He
threw up into the air an empty beer-bottle, so that it
revolved several times in its flight, and suddenly
catching it neck downward on the edge of a tray he
balanced it there for several seconds ; he juggled
four balls and two candles, catching the latter simultaneously in two candlesticks ; he played with a fan,
a wooden cigar and an umbrella, throwing them to
and fro in the air, and at last having the open umbrella
in his hand shielding his head, the cigar in his mouth,
and the fan coquettishly waving in his other hand.
Then he turned several somersaults on the mattress ;
did " the frog " ; tied himself into an American knot ;

walked on his hands, and having exhausted his little programme sent once more two kisses to the public, and, panting from the exercise, ran to grandfather to take his place at the organ.

Now was Arto's turn. This the dog perfectly well knew, and he had for some time been prancing round in excitement, and barking nervously. Perhaps the clever poodle wished to say that, in his opinion, it was unreasonable to go through acrobatic performances when Réaumur showed thirty-two degrees in the shade. But grandfather Lodishkin, with a cunning grin, pulled out of his coat-tail pocket a slender kizil switch. Arto's eyes took a melancholy expression. " Didn't I know it ! " they seemed to say, and he lazily and insubmissively raised himself on his hind paws, never once ceasing to look at his master and blink.

" Serve, Arto ! So, so, so . . .," ordered the old man, holding the switch over the poodle's head. " Over. So. Turn . . . again . . . again. . . . Dance, doggie, dance ! Sit ! Wha-at ? Don't want to ? Sit when you're told ! A-a. . . . That's right ! Now look ! Salute the respected public. Now, Arto ! " cried Lodishkin threateningly.

" Gaff ! " barked the poodle in disgust. Then he followed his master mournfully with his eyes, and added twice more, " Gaff, gaff."

" No, my old man doesn't understand me," this discontented barking seemed to say.

" That's it, that's better. Politeness before everything. Now we'll have a little jump," continued the old man, holding out the twig at a short distance above the ground. *"Allez !* There's nothing to hang out your tongue about, brother. *Allez!* Gop ! Splendid ! And now, please, *noch ein mal* . . . *Allez!* . . . Gop ! *Allez!* Gop ! Wonderful doggie. When you get home you shall have carrots. You don't like carrots, eh ? Ah, I'd completely forgotten. Then take my silk topper and ask the folk. P'raps they'll give you something a little more tasty."

Grandfather raised the dog on his hind legs and put in his mouth the old greasy cap which, with such delicate irony, he had named a silk topper. Arto, standing affectedly on his grey hind legs, and holding the cap in his teeth, came up to the terrace. In the hands of the delicate lady there appeared a small mother-of-pearl purse. All those around her smiled sympathetically.

" What ? Didn't I tell you ? " asked the old man of Sergey, teasingly. " Ask me if you ever want to know anything, brother, for I *know*. Nothing less than a rouble."

At that moment there broke out such an inhuman yowl that Arto involuntarily dropped the cap and leapt off with his tail between his legs, looked over his shoulders fearfully, and came and lay down at his master's feet.

" I wa-a-a-nt him," cried the curly-headed boy, stamping his feet. " Give him to me ! I want him. The dog, I tell you ! Trilly wa-ants the do-og ! "

" Ah, God in heaven ! Ah, Nikolai Apollonovitch ! . . . Little father, master ! . . . Be calm, Trilly, I beseech you," cried the voices of the people.

" The dog ! Give me the dog ; I want him ! Scum, demons, fatheads ! " cried the boy, fairly out of his mind.

" But, angel mine, don't upset your nerves," lisped the lady in the blue dressing-jacket. " You'd like to stroke the doggie ? Very well, very well, my joy, in a minute you shall. Doctor, what do you think, might Trilly stroke this dog ? "

" Generally speaking, I should not advise it," said the doctor, waving his hands. " But if we had some reliable disinfectant as, for instance, boracic acid or a weak solution of carbolic, then . . . generally . . ."

" The do-og ! "

" In a minute, my charmer, in a minute. So, doctor, you order that we wash the dog with boracic acid, and then. . . . Oh, Trilly, don't get into such a state ! Old man, bring up your dog, will you, if you please. Don't be afraid, you will be paid for it. And, listen a moment—is the dog ill ? I wish to ask, is the dog suffering from hydrophobia or skin disease ? "

" Don't want to stroke him, don't want to," roared Trilly, blowing out his mouth like a bladder. " Fatheads ! Demons ! Give it to me altogether ! I want to play with it. . . . For always."

" Listen, old man, come up here," cried the lady, trying to outshout the child. " Ah, Trilly, you'll kill your own mother if you make such a noise. Why ever did they let these music people in ? Come nearer —nearer still ; come when you're told ! . . . That's better. . . . Oh, don't take offence ! Trilly, your mother will do all that you ask. I beseech you, miss, do try and calm the child. . . . Doctor, I pray you. . . . How much d'you want, old man ? "

Grandfather removed his cap, and his face took on a respectfully piteous expression.

" As much as your kindness will think fit, my lady,

your Excellency. . . . We are people in a small way, and anything is a blessing for us. . . . Probably you will not do anything to offend an old man. . . ."

" Ah, how senseless ! Trilly, you'll make your little throat ache. . . . Don't you grasp the fact that the dog is *yours* and not mine. . . . Now, how much do you say ? Ten ? Fifteen ? Twenty ? "

" A-a-a ; I wa-ant it, give me the dog, give me the dog," squealed the boy, kicking the round stomach of the lackey who happened to be near.

" That is . . . forgive me, your Serenity," stuttered Lodishkin. " You see, I'm an old man, stupid. . . . It's difficult to understand at once. . . . What's more, I'm a bit deaf . . . so I ought to ask, in short, what were you wishing to say ? . . . For the dog ? . . ."

" Ah, God in heaven ! It seems to me you're playing the idiot on purpose," said the lady, boiling over. " Nurse, give Trilly some water at once ! I ask you, in the Russian language, for how much do you wish to sell your dog ? Do you understand— your dog, dog ? . . ."

" The dog ! The do-og ! " cried the boy, louder than ever.

Lodishkin took offence, and put his hat on again.

" Dogs, my lady, I do not sell," said he coldly and with dignity. " And, what is more, madam, that dog, it ought to be understood, has been for us two "—he pointed with his middle finger over his shoulder at Sergey—" has been for us two, feeder and clother. It has fed us, given us drink, and clothed us. I could not think of anything more impossible than, for example, that we should sell it."

Trilly all the while was giving forth piercing shrieks

like the whistle of a steam-engine. They gave him a glass of water, but he splashed it furiously all over the face of his governess.

" Listen, you crazy old man ! . . . There are no things which are not for sale, if only a large enough price be offered," insisted the lady, pressing her palms to her temples. " Miss, wipe your face quickly and give me my headache mixture. Now, perhaps your dog costs a hundred roubles ! What then, two hundred ? Three hundred ? Now answer, image. Doctor, for the love of the Lord, do say something to him ! "

" Pack up, Sergey," growled Lodishkin morosely. " Image, im-a-age. . . . Here, Arto ! . . ."

" Hey, wait a minute, if you please," drawled the stout gentleman in the gold spectacles in an authoritative bass. " You'd better not be obstinate, dear man, now I'm telling you. For your dog, ten roubles would be a beautiful price, and even for you into the bargain. . . . Just consider, ass, how much the lady is offering you."

" I most humbly thank you, sir," mumbled Lodishkin, hitching his organ on to his shoulders. " Only I can't see how such a piece of business could ever be done, as, for instance, to sell. Now, I should think you'd better seek some other dog somewhere else. . . . So good day to you. . . . Now, Sergey, go ahead ! "

" And have you got a passport ? " roared the doctor in a rage. " I know you—*canaille*."

" Porter ! Semyon ! Drive them out ! " cried the lady, her face distorted with rage.

The gloomy-looking porter in the rose-coloured

blouse rushed threateningly towards the artistes.
A great hubbub arose on the terrace, Trilly roaring
for all he was worth, his mother sobbing, the nurse
chattering volubly to her assistant, the doctor booming
like an angry cockchafer. But grandfather and
Sergey had no time to look back or to see how all
would end. The poodle running in front of them,
they got quickly to the gates, and after them came
the yard porter, punching the old man in the back,
beating on his organ, and crying out :

" Out you get, you rascals ! Thank God that
you're not hanging by your neck, you old scoundrel.
Remember, next time you come here, we shan't
stand on ceremony with you, but lug you at once to
the police station. Charlatans ! "

For a long time the boy and the old man walked
along silently together, but suddenly, as if they had
arranged the time beforehand, they both looked at
one another and laughed. Sergey simply burst into
laughter, and then Lodishkin smiled, seemingly in
some confusion.

" Eh, grandfather Lodishkin, you know everything ? " teased Sergey.

" Ye-s brother, we've been nicely fooled, haven't
we," said the old organ grinder, nodding his head.
" A nasty bit of a boy, however. . . . How they'll
bring up such a creature, the Lord only knows. Yes,
if you please, twenty-five men and women standing
around him, dancing dances for his sake. Well, if
he'd been in my power, I'd have taught him a lesson.
' Give me the dog,' says he. What then ? If he asks
for the moon out of the sky, give him that also, I
suppose. Come here, Arto, come here, my little

doggie doggie. Well, and what money we've taken to-day—astonishing ! "

" Better than money," continued Sergey, " one lady gave us clothes, another a whole rouble. And doesn't grandfather Lodishkin know everything in advance ? "

" You be quiet," growled the old man good-naturedly. " Don't you remember how you ran from the porter ? I thought I should never catch you up. A serious man, that porter ! "

Leaving the villas, the wandering troupe stepped downward by a steep and winding path to the sea. At this point the mountains, retiring from the shore, left a beautiful level beach covered with tiny pebbles, which lisped and chattered as the waves turned them over. Two hundred yards out to sea dolphins turned somersaults, showing for moments their curved and glimmering backs. Away on the horizon of the wide blue sea, standing as it were on a lovely velvet ribbon of dark purple, were the sails of fishing boats, tinted to a rose colour by the sunlight.

" Here we shall bathe, grandfather Lodishkin," said Sergey decisively. And he took off his trousers as he walked, jumping from one leg to the other to do so. " Let me help you to take off the organ."

He swiftly undressed, smacking his sunburnt body with the palms of his hands, ran down to the waves, took a handful of foam to throw over his shoulders, and jumped into the sea.

Grandfather undressed without hurry. Shielding his eyes from the sun with his hands, and wrinkling his brows, he looked at Sergey and grinned knowingly.

" He's not bad ; the boy is growing," thought

Lodishkin to himself. "Plenty of bones—all his ribs showing; but all the same, he'll be a strong fellow."

"Hey, Serozhska, don't you get going too far. A sea pig'll drag you off!"

"If so, I'll catch it by the tail," cried Sergey from a distance.

Grandfather stood a long time in the sunshine, feeling himself under his armpits. He went down to the water very cautiously, and before going right in, carefully wetted his bald red crown and the sunken sides of his body. He was yellow, wizened and feeble, his feet were astonishingly thin, and his back, with sharp protruding shoulder-blades, was humped by the long carrying of the organ.

"Look, grandfather Lodishkin!" cried Sergey, and he turned a somersault in the water.

Grandfather, who had now gone into the water up to his middle, sat down with a murmur of pleasure, and cried out to Sergey:

"Now, don't you play about, piggy. Mind what I tell you or I'll give it you."

Arto barked unceasingly, and jumped about the shore. He was very much upset to see the boy swimming out so far. "What's the use of showing off one's bravery?" worried the poodle. "Isn't there the earth, and isn't that good enough to go on, and much calmer?"

He went into the water two or three times himself, and lapped the waves with his tongue. But he didn't like the salt water, and was afraid of the little waves rolling over the pebbles towards him. He jumped back to dry sand, and at once set himself to bark at Sergey. "Why these silly, silly tricks? Why not come and sit down on the beach by the side of the old man? Dear, dear, what a lot of anxiety that boy does give us!"

"Hey, Serozha, time to come out, anyway. You've had enough," cried the old man.

"In a minute, grandfather Lodishkin," the boy cried back. "Just look how I do the steamboat. U-u-u-ukh!"

At last he swam in to the shore, but, before dressing, he caught Arto in his arms, and returning with him to the water's edge, flung him as far as he could. The dog at once swam back, leaving above the surface of the water his nostrils and floating ears alone, and snorting loudly and offendedly. Reaching dry sand, he shook his whole body violently, and clouds of water flew on the old man and on Sergey.

"Serozha, boy, look, surely that's for us!" said Lodishkin suddenly, staring upwards towards the cliff.

Along the downward path they saw that same gloomy-looking yard porter in the rose-coloured blouse with the speckled pattern, waving his arms and crying out to them, though they could not make out what he was saying, the same fellow who, a quarter of an hour ago, had driven the vagabond troupe from the villa.

"What does he want?" asked grandfather mistrustfully.

IV

The porter continued to cry, and at the same time to leap awkwardly down the steep path, the sleeves of his blouse trembling in the wind and the body of it blown out like a sail.

" O-ho-ho !   Wait, you three ! "

" There's no finishing with these people," growled Lodishkin angrily. " It's Artoshka they're after again."

" Grandfather, what d'you say ? Let's pitch into him ! " proposed Sergey bravely.

" You be quiet ! Don't be rash ! But what sort of people can they be ? God forgive us. . . ."

" I say, this is what you've got to do . . .," began the panting porter from afar. " You'll sell that dog. Eh, what ? There's no peace with the little master. Roars like a calf : ' Give me, give me the dog. . . .' The mistress has sent. ' Buy it,' says she, ' however much you have to pay.' "

" Now that's pretty stupid on your mistress's part," cried Lodishkin angrily, for he felt considerably more sure of himself here on the shore than he did in somebody else's garden. " And I should like to ask how can she be my mistress ? She's your mistress, perhaps, but to me further off than a third cousin, and I can spit at her if I want to. And now, please, for the love of God . . . I pray you . . . be so good as to go away . . . and leave us alone."

But the porter paid no attention. He sat down on the pebbles beside the old man, and, awkwardly scratching the back of his neck with his fingers, addressed him thus :

" Now, don't you grasp, fool ? . . ."

" I hear it from a fool," interrupted the old man.

" Now, come . . . that's not the point. . . . Just put it to yourself. What's the dog to you ? Choose another puppy ; all your expense is a stick, and there you have your dog again. Isn't that sense ? Don't I speak the truth ? Eh ? "

Grandfather meditatively fastened the strap which served him as a belt. To the obstinate questions of the porter he replied with studied indifference.

" Talk on, say all you've got to say, and then I'll answer you at once."

" Then, brother, think of the number," cried the porter hotly. " Two hundred, perhaps three hundred roubles in a lump ! Well, they generally give me something for my work . . . but just you think of it. Three whole hundred ! Why, you know, you could open a grocer's shop with that. . . ."

Whilst saying this the porter plucked from his pocket a piece of sausage, and threw it to the poodle. Arto caught it in the air, swallowed it at a gulp, and ingratiatingly wagged his tail.

" Finished ? " asked Lodishkin sweetly.

" Doesn't take long to say what I had to say. Give the dog, and the money will be in your hands."

" So-o," drawled grandfather mockingly. " That means the sale of the dog, I suppose ? "

" What else ? Just an ordinary sale. You see, our little master is so crazy. That's what's the matter. Whatever he wants, he turns the whole house upside down. ' Give,' says he, and it has to be given. That's how it is without his father. When his father's here . . . holy Saints ! . . . we all walk on our heads. The father is an engineer ; perhaps you've heard of Mr. Obolyaninof ? He builds railway lines all over Russia. A millionaire ! They've only one boy, and they spoil him. ' I want a live pony,' says he—here's a pony for you. 'I want a boat,' says he—here's a real boat. There is nothing that they refuse him. . . ."

" And the moon ? "

" That is, in what sense ? " asked the porter.

" I say, has he never asked for the moon from the sky ? "

" The moon. What nonsense is that ? " said the porter, turning red. " But come now, we're agreed, aren't we, dear man ? "

By this time grandfather had succeeded in putting on his old green-seamed jacket, and he drew himself up as straight as his bent back would permit.

" I'll ask you one thing, young man," said he, not without dignity. " If you had a brother, or, let us say, a friend, that had grown up with you from child-hood—Now stop, friend, don't throw sausage to the dog . . . better eat it yourself. . . . You can't bribe the dog with that, brother—I say, if you had a friend, the best and truest friend that it's possible to have . . . one who from childhood . . . well, then, for example, for how much would you sell him ? "

" I'd find a price even for him ! . . ."

" Oh, you'd find a price. Then go and tell your master who builds the railroads," cried grandfather in a loud voice—" Go and tell him that not everything that ordinarily is for sale is also to be bought. Yes ! And you'd better not stroke the dog. That's to no purpose. Here, Arto, dog, I'll give it you. Come on, Sergey."

" Oh, you old fool ! " cried the porter at last.

" Fool ; yes, I was one from birth, but you, bit of rabble, Judas, soul-seller ! " shouted Lodishkin. " When you see your lady-general, give her our kind respects, our deepest respects. Sergey, roll up the mattress. Ai, ai, my back, how it aches! Come on."

"So-o, that's what it means," drawled the porter significantly.

"Yes. That's what it is. Take it!" answered the old man exasperatingly. The troupe then wandered off along the shore, following on the same road. Once, looking back accidentally, Sergey noticed that the porter was following them; his face seemed cogitative and gloomy, his cap was over his eyes, and he scratched with five fingers his shaggy carrotty-haired neck.

V

A certain spot between Miskhor and Aloopka had long since been put down by Lodishkin as a splendid place for having lunch, and it was to this that they journeyed now. Not far from a bridge over a rushing mountain torrent there wandered from the cliff side a cold chattering stream of limpid water. This was in the shade of crooked oak trees and thick hazel bushes. The stream had made itself a shallow basin in the earth, and from this overflowed, in tiny snake-like streamlets, glittering in the grass like living silver. Every morning and evening one might see here pious Turks making their ablutions and saying their prayers.

"Our sins are heavy and our provisions are meagre," said grandfather, sitting in the shade of a hazel bush. "Now, Serozha, come along. Lord, give Thy blessing!"

He pulled out from a sack some bread, some tomatoes, a lump of Bessarabian cheese, and a bottle of olive oil. He brought out a little bag of salt, an old rag tied round with string. Before eating, the old man crossed himself many times and whispered something. Then he broke the crust of bread into three unequal parts: the largest he gave to Sergey (he is growing—he must eat), the next largest he gave to the poodle, and the smallest he took for himself.

"In the name of the Father and the Son. The eyes of all wait upon Thee, O Lord," whispered he, making a salad of the tomatoes. "Eat, Serozha!"

They ate slowly, not hurrying, in silence, as people eat who work. All that was audible was the working of three pairs of jaws. Arto, stretched on his stomach, ate his little bit at one side, gnawing the crust of bread, which he held between his front paws. Grandfather and Sergey alternately dipped their tomatoes in the salt, and made their lips and hands red with the juice. When they had finished they drank water from the stream, filling a little tin can and putting it to their mouths. It was fine water, and so cold that the mug went cloudy on the outside from the moisture condensing on it. The mid-day heat and the long road had tired the performers, for they had been up with the sun. Grandfather's eyes closed involuntarily. Sergey yawned and stretched himself.

"Well now, little brother, what if we were to lie down and sleep for a minute or so?" asked grandfather. "One last drink of water. Ukh! Fine!" cried he, taking his lips from the can and breathing heavily, the bright drops of water running from his beard and whiskers. "If I were Tsar I'd drink that water every day . . . from morning to night. Here, Arto! Well, God has fed us and nobody has seen us, or if

anybody has seen us he hasn't taken offence. . . .
Okh—okh—okhonush—kee—ee ! "

The old man and the boy lay down side by side in
the grass, making pillows for their heads of their
jackets. The dark leaves of the rugged many-
branching oaks murmured above them ; occasionally
through the shade gleamed patches of bright blue sky ;
the little streams running from stone to stone chattered
monotonously and stealthily as if they were putting
someone to sleep by sorcery. Grandfather turned
from side to side, muttered something to Sergey,
but to Sergey his voice seemed far away in a soft and
sleepy distance, and the words were strange, as those
spoken in a fairy tale.

" First of all—I buy you a costume, rose and gold
. . . slippers also of rose-coloured satin . . . in Kief or
Kharkof, or, perhaps, let us say in the town of Odessa
—there, brother, there are circuses, if you like ! . . .
Endless lanterns . . . all electricity. . . . People,
perhaps five thousand, perhaps more . . . how should
I know. We should have to make up a name for you
—an Italian name, of course. What can one do with a
name like Esteepheyef, or let us say, Lodishkin ?
Quite absurd ! No imagination in them whatever.
So we'd let you go on the placards as Antonio, or
perhaps, also quite good, Enrico or Alphonso. . . ."

The boy heard no more. A sweet and gentle
slumber settled down upon him and took possession
of his body. And grandfather fell asleep, losing
suddenly the thread of his favourite after-dinner
thoughts, his dream of Sergey's magnificent acrobatic
future. Once, however, in his dream it appeared to
him that Arto was growling at somebody. For a

L 2

moment through his dreamy brain there passed the half-conscious and alarming remembrance of the porter in the rose-coloured blouse, but overcome with sleep, tiredness and heat, he could not get up, but only idly, with closed eyes, cried out to the dog :

" Arto . . . where're you going ?   I'll g-give it you, gipsy ! "

But at once he forgot what he was talking about, and his mind fell back into the heaviness of sleep and vague dreams.

At last the voice of Sergey woke him up, for the boy was running to and fro just beyond the stream, shouting loudly and whistling, calling anxiously for the dog.

" Here, Arto ! Come back ! Pheu, pheu ! Come back, Arto ! "

" What are you howling about, Sergey ? " cried Lodishkin in a tone of displeasure, trying to bring the circulation back to a sleeping arm.

" We've lost the dog whilst we slept.   That's what we've done," answered the boy in a harsh, scolding note.   " The dog's lost."

He whistled again sharply, and cried :

" Arto-o-o ! "

" Ah, you're just making up nonsense ! He'll return," said grandfather.   But all the same, he also got up and began to call the dog in an angry, sleepy, old man's falsetto :

" Arto !   Here, dog ! "

The old man hurriedly and tremblingly ran across the bridge and began to go upward along the highway, calling the dog as he went.   In front of him lay the bright, white stripe of the road, level and clear for half a mile, but on it not a figure, not a shadow.

" Arto ! Ar-tosh-enka ! " wailed the old man in a piteous voice, but suddenly he stopped calling him, bent down on the roadside and sat on his heels.

" Yes, that's what it is," said the old man in a failing voice. " Sergey ! Serozha ! Come here, my boy ! "

" Now what do you want ? " cried the boy rudely. " What have you found now ? Found yesterday lying by the roadside, eh ? "

" Serozha . . . what is it ? . . . What do you make of it ? Do you see what it is ? " asked the old man, scarcely above a whisper. He looked at the boy in a piteous and distracted way, and his arms hung help-lessly at his sides.

In the dust of the road lay a comparatively large half-eaten lump of sausage, and about it in all directions were printed a dog's paw-marks.

" He's drawn it off, the scoundrel, lured it away," whispered grandfather in a frightened shiver, still sitting on his heels. " It's he ; no one else, it's quite clear. Don't you remember how he threw the sausage to Arto down by the sea ? "

" Yes, it's quite clear," repeated Sergey sulkily.

Grandfather's wide-open eyes filled with tears, quickly overflowing down his cheeks. He hid them with his hands.

" Now, what can we do Serozhenka ? Eh, boy ? What can we do now ? " asked the old man, rocking to and fro and weeping helplessly.

" Wha-at to do, wha-at to do ! " teased Sergey. " Get up, grandfather Lodishkin ; let's be going ! "

" Yes, let us go ! " repeated the old man sadly and humbly, raising himself from the ground. " We'd better be going, I suppose, Serozhenka."

Losing patience, Sergey began to scold the old man as if he were a little boy.

" That's enough drivelling, old man, stupid ! Who ever heard of people taking away other folks' dogs in this way ? It's not the law. What-ye blinking your eyes at me for ? Is what I say untrue ? Let us go simply and say, ' Give us back the dog ! ' and if they won't give it, then to the courts with it, and there's an end of it."

" To the courts . . . yes . . . of course. . . . That's correct, to the courts, of course . . . ," repeated Lodishkin, with a senseless bitter smile. But his eyes looked hither and thither in confusion. " To the courts . . . yes . . . only you know, Serozhenka . . . it wouldn't work . . . we'd never get to the courts. . . ."

" How not work ? The law is the same for everybody. What have they got to say for themselves ? " interrupted the boy impatiently.

" Now, Serozha, don't do that . . . don't be angry with me. They won't give us back the dog." At this point grandfather lowered his voice in a mysterious way. " I fear, on account of the passport. Didn't you hear what the gentleman said up there ? ' Have you a passport ? ' he says. Well, and there, you see, I,"—here grandfather made a wry and seemingly frightened face, and whispered barely audibly—" I'm living with somebody else's passport, Serozha."

" How somebody else's ? "

" Somebody else's. There's no more about it. I

lost my own at Taganrog. Perhaps somebody stole it.
For two years after that I wandered about, hid myself,
gave bribes, wrote petitions . . . at last I saw there
was no getting out of it. I had to live like a hare—
afraid of everything. But once in Odessa, in a night
house, a Greek remarked to me the following :—
' What you say,' says he, ' is nonsense. Put twenty-
five roubles on the table, and I'll give you a passport
that'll last you till doomsday.' I worried my brain
about that. ' I'll lose my head for this,' I thought.
However, ' Give it me,' said I. And from that time,
my dear boy, I've been going about the world with
another man's passport."

" Ah, grandfather, grandfather ! " sighed Sergey,
with tears in his eyes. " I'm sorry about the dog.
It's a very fine dog, you know. . . ."

" Serozhenka, my darling," cried the old man
trembling. " If only I had a real passport. Do you
think it would matter to me even if they were
generals? I'd take them by the throat ! . . . How's
this ? One minute, if you please ! What right have
you to steal other people's dogs ? What law is there
for that ? But now there's a stopper on us, Serozha.
If I go to the police station the first thing will be,
' Show us your passport ! Are you a citizen of Samara,
by name Martin Lodishkin ? ' I, your Excellency,
dear me—I, little brother, am not Lodishkin at all,
and not a citizen, but a peasant. Ivan Dudkin is my
name. And who that Lodishkin might be, God alone
knows ! How can I tell ? Perhaps a thief or an
escaped convict. Perhaps even a murderer. No,
Serozha, we shouldn't effect anything that way.
Nothing at all. . . ."

Grandfather choked, and tears trickled once more over his sunburnt wrinkles. Sergey, who had listened to the old man in silence, his brows tightly knit, his face pale with agitation, suddenly stood up and cried : " Come on, grandfather. To the devil with the passport ! I suppose we don't intend to spend the night here on the high road ? "

" Ah, my dear, my darling," said the old man, trembling. " 'Twas a clever dog . . . that Artoshenka of ours. We shan't find such another. . . ."

" All right, all right. Get up ! " cried Sergey imperiously. " Now let me knock the dust off you. I feel quite worn out, grandfather."

They worked no more that day. Despite his youthful years, Sergey well understood the fateful meaning of the dreadful word " passport." So he sought no longer to get Arto back, either through the courts or in any other decisive way. And as he walked along the road with grandfather towards the inn, where they should sleep, his face took on a new, obstinate, concentrated expression, as if he had just thought out something extraordinarily serious and great.

Without actually expressing their intention, the two wanderers made a considerable detour in order to pass once more by Friendship Villa, and they stopped for a little while outside the gates, in the vague hope of catching a glimpse of Arto, or of hearing his bark from afar. But the iron gates of the magnificent villa were bolted and locked, and an important, undisturbed and solemn stillness reigned over the shady garden under the sad and mighty cypresses.

" Peo-ple ! " cried the old man in a quavering

voice, putting into that one word all the burning grief that filled his heart.

" Ah, that's enough. Come on ! " cried the boy roughly, pulling his companion by the sleeve.

" Serozhenka ! Don't you think there's a chance that Artoshenka might run away from them ? " sighed the old man. " Eh ! What do you think, dear ? "

But the boy did not answer the old man. He went ahead in firm large strides, his eyes obstinately fixed on the road, his brows obstinately frowning.

VI

They reached Aloopka in silence. Grandfather muttered to himself and sighed the whole way. Sergey preserved in his face an angry and resolute expression. They stopped for the night at a dirty Turkish coffee-house, bearing the splendid name of Eeldeez, which means in Turkish, a star. In the same room with them slept Greek stone-breakers, Turkish ditch-diggers, a gang of Russian workmen, and several dark-faced, mysterious tramps, the sort of which there are so many wandering about Southern Russia. Directly the coffee-house closed they stretched themselves out on the benches along the length of the walls, or simply upon the floor, and the more experienced placed their possessions and their clothes in a bundle under their heads.

It was long after midnight when Sergey, who had been lying side by side with grandfather on the floor, got up stealthily and began to dress himself without noise. Through the wide window-panes poured the full light of the moon, falling on the floor to make a trembling carpet of silver, and giving to the faces of the sleepers an expression of suffering and death.

" Where's you going to, zis time o' night ? " cried the owner of the coffee-house, Ibrahim, a young Turk lying at the door of the shop.

" Let me pass ; it's necessary. I've got to go out," answered Sergey in a harsh, business-like tone. " Get up, Turco ! "

Yawning and stretching himself, Ibrahim got up and opened the door, clicking his tongue reproachfully. The narrow streets of the Tartar *bazar* were enveloped in a dense dark-blue mist, which covered with a tooth-shaped design the whole cobbled roadway ; one side of the street lay in shade, the other, with all its white-walled houses, was illumined by the moonlight. Dogs were barking at distant points of the village. Somewhere on the upper high road horses were trotting, and the metallic clink of their hoofs sounded in the night stillness.

Passing the white mosque with its green cupola, surrounded by its grove of silent cypresses, Sergey tripped along a narrow, crooked lane to the great highway. In order that he might run quickly the boy was practically in his undergarments only. The moon shone on him from behind, and his shadow ran ahead in a strange foreshortened silhouette. There were mysterious shaggy shrubs on each side of the road, a bird was crying monotonously from the bushes in a gentle, tender tone " *Splew ! Splew !* "[1] and it seemed as if it thought itself to be a sentry in the night silence, guarding some melancholy secret, and powerlessly struggling with sleep and tiredness, com-

[1] The word " splew " is Russian for " I sleep."

plaining hopelessly, quietly, to someone, *" Splew,
splew,* I sleep, I sleep."

And over the dark bushes, over the blue head-dress
of the distant forests, rose with its two peaks to the
sky, Ai-Petri—so light, so clear-cut, so ethereal, as if it
were something cut from a gigantic piece of silver
cardboard in the sky. Sergey felt a little depressed
by the majestic silence in which his footsteps sounded
so distinctly and daringly, but at the same time there
rose in his heart a sort of ticklish, head-whirling,
spirit of adventure. At a turn of the road the sea
suddenly opened before him, immense and calm,
quietly and solemnly breaking on the shore. From the
horizon to the beach stretched a narrow, a quivering,
silver roadway ; in the midst of the sea this roadway
was lost, and only here and there the traces of it
glittered, but suddenly nearer the shore it became a
wide flood of living, glimmering metal, ornamenting
the coast like a belt of deep lace.

Sergey slipped noiselessly through the wooden
gateway leading to the park. There, under the dense
foliage of the trees, it was quite dark. From afar
sounded the ceaseless murmur of mountain streams,
and one could feel their damp cold breath. The
wooden planks of the bridge clacked soundingly as he
ran across ; the water beneath looked dark and
dreadful. In a moment he saw in front of him the
high gates with their lace pattern of iron, and the
creeping gloxinia hanging over them. The moonlight,
pouring from a gap in the trees, outlined the lacework
of the iron gates with, as it were, a gentle phospho-
rescence. On the other side of the gates it was dark,
and there was a terrifying stillness.

Sergey hesitated for some moments, feeling in his soul some doubt, even a little fear. But he conquered his feelings and whispered obstinately to himself :

" All the same ; I'm going to climb in, all the same ¦ "

The elegant cast-iron design furnished solid stepping places and holding places for the muscular arms and feet of the climber. But over the gateway, at a considerable height, and fitting to the gates, was a broad archway of stone. Sergey felt all over this with his hands, and climbed up on to it, lay on his stomach, and tried to let himself down on the other side. He hung by his hands, but could find no catching place for his feet. The stone archway stood out too far from the gate for his legs to reach, so he dangled there, and as he couldn't get back, his body grew limp and heavy, and terror possessed his soul.

At last he could hold on no longer ; his fingers gave, and he slipped and fell violently to the ground.

He heard the gravel crunch under him, and felt a sharp pain in his knees. He lay crouching on all fours for some moments, stunned by the fall. He felt that in a minute out would come the gloomy-looking porter, raise a cry and make a fearful to do. . . . But the same brooding and self-important silence reigned in the garden as before. Only a sort of strange monotonous buzzing sounded everywhere about the villa and the estate.

" Zhu . . . zhzhu . . . zhzhu. . . ."

" Ah, that's the noise in my ears," guessed Sergey. When he got on his feet again and looked round, all the garden had become dreadful and mysterious, and beautiful as in a fairy tale, a scented dream. On the flower-beds the flowers, barely visible in the darkness, leaned toward one another as if communicating a vague alarm. The magnificent dark-scented cypresses nodded pensively, and seemed to reflect reproachfully over all. And beyond a little stream the tired little bird struggled with its desire to slumber, and cried submissively and plaintively, " *Splew, splew*, I sleep, I sleep."

Sergey could not recognise the place in the darkness for the confusion of the paths and the shadows. He wandered for some time on the crunching gravel before he found the house.

He had never in his whole life felt such complete helplessness and torturesome loneliness and desolation as he did now. The immense house felt as if it must be full of concealed enemies watching him with wicked glee, peering at him from the dark windows. Every moment he expected to hear some sort of signal or wrathful fierce command.

" . . . Only not in the house . . . he couldn't possibly be in the house," whispered the boy to himself as in a dream ; " if they put him in the house he would begin to howl, and they'd soon get tired of it. . . ."

He walked right round the house. At the back, in the wide yard, were several outhouses more or less simple and capacious, evidently designed for the accommodation of servants. There was not a light in any of them, and none in the great house itself ; only the moon saw itself darkly in the dull dead windows. " I shan't ever get away from here ; no, never ! " thought Sergey to himself despairingly, and just for a moment his thoughts went back to the sleeping tavern and grandfather and the old organ, and to the place where they had slept in the afternoon, to their life of the road, and he whispered softly to himself, " Never, never any more of that again," and so thinking, his fear changed to a sort of calm and despairing conviction.

But then suddenly he became aware of a faint, far-off whimpering. The boy stood still as if spellbound, not daring to move. The whimpering sound was repeated. It seemed to come from the stone cellar near which Sergey was standing, and which was ventilated by a window with no glass, just four rough square openings. Stepping across a flower-bed, the boy went up to the wall, pressed his face to one of the openings, and whistled. He heard a slight cautious movement somewhere in the depths, and then all was silent.

" Arto, Artoshka ! " cried Sergey, in a trembling whisper.

At this there burst out at once a frantic burst of barking, filling the whole garden and echoing from all sides. In this barking there was expressed, not only joyful welcome, but piteous complaint and rage, and physical pain. One could hear how the dog was tugging and pulling at something in the dark cellar, trying to get free.

" Arto ! Doggikin ! . . . Artoshenka ! . . ." repeated the boy in a sobbing voice.

" Peace, cursed one ! Ah, you convict ! " cried a brutal bass voice from below.

There was a sound of beating from the cellar. The dog gave vent to a long howl.

" Don't dare to kill him ! Kill the dog if you dare, you villain ! " cried Sergey, quite beside himself, scratching the stone wall with his nails.

What happened after that Sergey only remembered confusedly, like something he had experienced in a dreadful nightmare. The door of the cellar opened wide with a noise, and out rushed the porter. He was only in his pantaloons, bare-footed, bearded, pale from the bright light of the moon, which was shining straight in his face. To Sergey he seemed like a giant or an enraged monster, escaped from a fairy tale.

" Who goes there ? I shall shoot. Thieves ! Robbers ! " thundered the voice of the porter.

At that moment, however, there rushed from the door of the cellar out into the darkness Arto, with a broken cord hanging from his neck.

There was no question of the boy following the dog. The sight of the porter filled him with supernatural terror, tied his feet, and seemed to paralyse his whole body. Fortunately, this state of nerves didn't last long. Almost involuntarily Sergey gave vent to a piercing and despairing shriek, and he took to his heels at random, not looking where he was going, and absolutely forgetting himself from fear.

He went off like a bird, his feet striking the ground as if they had suddenly become two steel springs, and by his side ran Arto, joyfully and effusively barking. After them came the porter, heavily, shouting and swearing at them as he went.

Sergey was making for the gate, but suddenly he had an intuition that there was no road for him that way. Along the white stone wall of the garden was a narrow track in the shelter of the cypress trees, and Sergey flung himself along this path, obedient to the one feeling of fright. The sharp needles of the cypress trees, pregnant with the smell of pitch, struck him in the face. He fell over some roots and hurt his arm so that the blood came, but jumped up at once, not even noticing the pain, and went on as fast as ever, bent double, and still followed by Arto.

So he ran along this narrow corridor, with the wall on one side and the closely ranged file of cypresses on the other, ran as might a crazy little forest animal feeling itself in an endless trap. His mouth grew dry, his breathing was like needles in his breast, yet all the time the noise of the following porter was audible, and the boy, losing his head, ran back to the gate again and then once more up the narrow pathway, and back again.

At last Sergey ran himself tired. Instead of the wild terror, he began to feel a cold, deadly melancholy, a tired indifference to danger. He sat down under a tree, and pressed his tired-out body to the trunk and closed his eyes. Nearer and nearer came the heavy steps of the enemy. Arto whimpered softly, putting his nose between the boy's knees.

Two steps from where Sergey sat a big branch of a tree bent downward. The boy, raising his eyes accidentally, was suddenly seized with joy and jumped to his feet at a bound, for he noticed that at the place where he was sitting the wall was very low, not more than a yard and a half in height. The top was plastered with lime and broken bottle-glass, but Sergey did not give that a thought. In the twinkling of an eye he grabbed Arto by the body, and lifting him up put him with his fore-legs on the top of the wall. The clever poodle understood perfectly, clambered on to the top, wagged his tail and barked triumphantly.

Sergey followed him, making use of the branches of the cypress, and he had hardly got on to the top of the wall before he caught sight of a large, shadowy face. Two supple, agile bodies—the dog's and the boy's — went quickly and softly to the bottom, on to the road, and following them, like a dirty stream, came the vile, malicious abuse of the porter.

But whether it was that the porter was less sure on his feet than our two friends, or was tired with running round the garden, or had simply given up hope of overtaking them, he followed them no further. Nevertheless, they ran on as fast as they could without resting, strong, light-footed, as if the joy of deliverance had given them wings. The poodle soon began to exhibit his accustomed frivolity. Sergey often looked back fearfully over his shoulders, but Arto leapt on him, wagging his ears ecstatically, and waving the bit of cord that was hanging from his neck, actually licking Sergey's face with his long tongue. The boy became calm only by the time they got to the spring where the afternoon before grandfather and he had made their lunch. There both the boy and the dog put their lips to the cold stream, and drank long and eagerly of the fresh and pleasant water. They got in one another's way with their heads, and thinking they had quenched their thirst, yet returned to the basin to drink more, and would not stop. When at last they got away from the spot the water rolled about in their overfull insides as they ran. The danger past, all the terrors of the night explored, they felt gay now, and light-hearted, going along the white road brightly lit up by the moon, going through the dark shrubs, now wet with morning dew, and exhaling the sweet scent of freshened leaves.

At the door of the coffee-house Eeldeez, Ibrahim met the boy and whispered reproachfully :

" Where's you been a-roving, boy ? Where's you been ? No, no, no, zat's not good. . . ."

Sergey did not wish to wake grandfather, but Arto did it for him. He at once found the old man in the midst of the other people sleeping on the floor, and quite forgetting himself, licked him all over his cheeks and eyes and nose and mouth, yelping joyfully. Grandfather awoke, saw the broken cord hanging from the poodle's neck, saw the boy lying beside him covered with dust, and understood all. He asked Sergey to explain, but got no answer. The little boy was asleep, his arms spread out on the floor, his mouth wide open.

X

THE ELEPHANT

THE little girl was unwell. Every day the doctor
came to see her, Dr. Michael Petrovitch, whom
she had known long, long ago. And sometimes he
brought with him two other doctors whom she didn't
know. They turned the little girl over on to her back
and then on to her stomach, listened to something,
putting an ear against her body, pulled down her
under eyelids and looked at them. They seemed
very important people, they had stern faces, and they
spoke to one another in a language the little girl did
not understand.

Afterwards they went out from the nursery into the
drawing-room, where mother sat waiting for them.
The most important doctor—the tall one with grey
hair and gold eye-glasses—talked earnestly to her for
a long time. The door was not shut, and the little
girl lying on her bed could see and hear all. There
was much that she didn't understand, but she knew
the talk was about her. Mother looked up at the
doctor with large, tired, tear-filled eyes. When the
doctors went away the chief one said loudly :

" The most important thing is—don't let her be
dull. Give in to all her whims."

" Ah, doctor, but she doesn't want anything ! "

" Well, I don't know . . . think what she used to like before she was ill. Toys . . . something nice to eat. . . ."

" No, no, doctor ; she doesn't want *anything*."

" Well, try and tempt her with something. . . . No matter what it is. . . . I give you my word that if you can only make her laugh and enjoy herself, it would be better than any medicine. You must understand that your daughter's illness is indifference to life, and nothing more. . . . Good morning, madam ! "

II

" Dear Nadya, my dear little girl," said mother ; " isn't there anything you would like to have ? "

" No, mother, I don't want anything."

" Wouldn't you like me to put out all your dolls on the bed ? We'll arrange the easy chair, the sofa, the little table, and put the tea-service out. The dolls shall have tea and talk to one another about the weather and their children's health."

" Thank you, mother. . . . I don't want it. . . . It's so dull. . . ."

" Oh, very well, little girlie, we won't have the dolls. Suppose we ask Katya or Zhenochka to come and see you. You're very fond of them."

" I don't want them, mother. Indeed, I don't. I don't want anything, don't want anything. I'm so dull ! "

" Shall I get you some chocolate ? "

But the little girl didn't answer, she lay and stared at the ceiling with steadfast, mournful eyes. She had no pain at all, she wasn't even feverish. But she was getting thinner and weaker every day. She didn't mind what was done to her; it made no difference, she didn't care for anything. She lay like this all day and all night, quiet, mournful. Sometimes she would doze for half an hour, and then in her dreams she would see something long and grey and dull, as if she were looking at rain in autumn.

When the door leading from the nursery into the drawing-room was open, and the other door into the study was open too, the little girl could see her father. Father would walk swiftly from one corner of the room to the other, and all the time he would smoke, smoke. Sometimes he would come into the nursery and sit on the edge of Nadya's bed and stroke her feet gently. Then he would get up suddenly and go to the window, whistle a little, and look out into the street, but his shoulders would tremble. He would hurriedly press his handkerchief first to one eye and then to the other, and then go back into his study as if he were angry. Then he would begin again to pace up and down and smoke . . . and smoke . . . and smoke. And his study would look all blue from the clouds of tobacco smoke.

III

One morning the little girl woke to feel a little stronger than usual. She had dreamed something, but she couldn't remember exactly what she had dreamed, and she looked attentively into her mother's eyes for a long time.

" What would you like ? " asked mother.

But the little girl had suddenly remembered her

dream, and she said in a whisper, as if it were a secret :

" Mother . . . could I have . . . an elephant ? Only not one that's painted in a picture. . . . Eh ? "

" Of course you can, my child, of course."

She went into the study and told papa that the little girl wanted an elephant. Papa put on his coat and hat directly, and went off somewhere. In half an hour he came back, bringing with him an expensive beautiful toy. It was a large grey elephant that could move its head and wave its tail ; on its back was a red saddle, and on the saddle there was a golden tent with three little men sitting inside. But the little girl paid no attention to the toy ; she only looked up at the walls and ceiling, and said languidly :

" No. That's not at all what I meant. I wanted a real live elephant, and this one's dead."

" But only look at it, Nadya," said mamma. " We'll wind him up, and he'll be exactly, exactly like a live one."

The elephant was wound up with a key, and it then began to move its legs and walk slowly along the table, nodding its head and waving its tail. But the little girl wasn't interested at all ; she was even bored by it, though in order that her father shouldn't feel hurt she whispered kindly :

" Thank you very very much, dear papa. I don't think anyone has such an interesting toy as this. . . . Only . . . you remember . . . long ago, you promised to take me to a menagerie to see a real elephant . . . and you didn't bring it here. . . ."

" But listen, my dear child. Don't you understand that that's impossible. An elephant is very big ; he's as high as the ceiling, and we couldn't get him into our rooms. And what's more, where could I obtain one? "

" Papa, I don't want such a big one. . . . You could bring me as little a one as you like, so long as it's alive. As big as this . . . a baby elephant."

" My dear child, I should be glad to do anything for you, but this is impossible. It's just as if you suddenly said to me, ' Papa, get me the sun out of the sky.' "

The little girl smiled sadly.

" How stupid you are, papa! As if I didn't know it's impossible to get the sun, it's all on fire. And the moon, too, you can't get. No, if only I had a little elephant . . . a real one."

And she quietly closed her eyes and whispered:

" I'm tired. . . . Forgive me, papa. . . ."

Papa clutched at his hair and ran away to his study, where for some time he marched up and down. Then he resolutely threw his unfinished cigarette on the floor—mamma was always grumbling at him about this—and called out to the maid:

" Olga! Bring me my hat and coat! "

His wife came out into the hall.

" Where are you going, Sasha? " asked she.

He breathed heavily as he buttoned up his coat.

" I don't know myself, Mashenka, where I'm going. . . . Only I think that this evening I shall actually bring a live elephant here.

His wife looked anxiously at him.

" My dear, are you quite well? " said she. " Haven't you got a headache? Perhaps you slept badly last night? "

" I didn't sleep at all," he answered angrily. " I

see, you want to ask if I'm going out of my mind. Not just yet. Good-bye. You'll see this evening."

And he went off, loudly slamming the front door after him.

IV

In two hours' time he was seated in the front row at the menagerie, and watching trained animals perform their different parts under the direction of the manager. Clever dogs jumped, turned somersaults, danced, sang to music, made words with large cardboard letters. Monkeys—one in a red skirt, the other in blue knickers—walked the tight rope and rode upon a large poodle. An immense tawny lion jumped through burning hoops. A clumsy seal fired a pistol. And at last they brought out the elephants. There were three of them : one large and two quite small ones, dwarfs ; but all the same, much larger than a horse. It was strange to see how these enormous animals, apparently so heavy and awkward, could perform the most difficult tricks which would be out of the power of a very skilful man. The largest elephant distinguished himself particularly. He stood up at first on his hind legs, then sat down, then stood on his head with his feet in the air, walked along wooden bottles, then on a rolling cask, turned over the pages of a large picture-book with his tail, and, finally, sat down at a table and, tying a serviette round his neck, had his dinner just like a well-brought-up little boy.

The show came to an end. The spectators went out. Nadya's father went up to the stout German, the manager of the menagerie. He was standing behind a partition smoking a long black cigar.

" Pardon me, please," said Nadya's father. " Would it be possible for you to send your elephant to my house for a short time ? "

The German's eyes opened wide in astonishment, and his mouth also, so that the cigar fell to the ground. He made an exclamation, bent down, picked up the cigar, put it in his mouth again, and then said :

" Send ? The elephant ? To your house ? I don't understand you."

It was evident from his look that he also wanted to ask Nadya's father if he were a little wrong in the head. . . . But the father quickly began to explain the matter : his only daughter, Nadya, was ill with a strange malady which no doctor could understand nor cure. She had lain for a month in her bed, had grown thinner and weaker every day, wasn't interested in anything, was only dull—she seemed to be slowly dying. The doctors had said she must be roused, but she didn't care for anything ; they had said that all her desires were to be gratified, but she didn't wish for anything at all. To-day she had said she wanted to see a live elephant. Wasn't it possible to manage that she should ?

And he took the German by the button of his coat, and added in a trembling voice :

" Well . . . of course I hope that my little girl will get well again. But suppose . . . God forbid it ! . . . her illness should take a sudden turn for the worse . . . and she should die ! Just think—shouldn't I be tortured for all the rest of my life to think that I hadn't fulfilled her last, her very last wish ! "

The German wrinkled up his forehead and thoughtfully scratched his left eyebrow with his little finger. At length he asked :

" H'm. . . . And how old is your little girl ? "

" Six."

" H'm. . . . My Lisa's six, too. H'm. But you know, it'll cost you a lot. We'll have to take the elephant one night, and we can't bring it back till the next night. It'll be impossible to do it in the day-time. There'd be such crowds of people, and such a fuss. . . . It means that I should lose a whole day, and you ought to pay me for it."

" Of course, of course . . . don't be anxious about that."

" And then : will the police allow an elephant to be taken into a private house ? "

" I'll arrange it. They'll allow it."

" And there's another question : will the landlord of your house allow the elephant to come in ? "

" Yes. I'm my own landlord."

" Aha ! That's all the better. And still another question : what floor do you live on ? "

" The second."

" H'm. . . . That's not so good. . . . Have you a broad staircase, a high ceiling, a large room, wide doorways, and a very stout flooring. Because my ' Tommy ' is three and a quarter arshins in height and five and a half long. And he weighs a hundred and twelve poods." [1]

Nadya's father thought for a moment.

" Do you know what ? " said he. " You come with me and look at the place. If it's necessary, I'll have a wider entrance made."

[1] An arshin is about ¾ of a yard, and a pood is 36 lbs.

"Very good!" agreed the manager of the menagerie.

V

That night they brought the elephant to visit the sick girl.

He marched importantly down the very middle of the street, nodding his head and curling up and uncurling his trunk. A great crowd of people came with him, in spite of the late hour. But the elephant paid no attention to the people; he saw hundreds of them every day in the menagerie. Only once did he get a little angry. A street urchin ran up to him under his very legs, and began to make grimaces for the diversion of the sight-seers.

Then the elephant quietly took off the boy's cap with his trunk and threw it over a wall near by, which was protected at the top by projecting nails.

A policeman came up to the people and tried to persuade them:

"Gentlemen, I beg you to go away. What's there here unusual? I'm astonished at you! As if you never saw an elephant in the street before."

They came up to the house. On the staircase, and all the way up to the dining-room where the elephant was to go, every door was opened wide; the latches had all been pushed down with a hammer. It was just the same as had been done once when they brought a large wonder-working ikon into the house.

But when he came to the staircase the elephant stopped in alarm, and refused to go on.

"You must get him some dainty to eat," said the

German. . . . " A sweet cake or something. . . . But . . . Tommy ! . . . Oho-ho . . . Tommy ! "

Nadya's father ran off to a neighbouring confectioner's and bought a large round pistachio tart. The elephant looked as if he would like to eat it at one gulp, and the cardboard box it was in as well, but the German gave him only a quarter of the tart. . . . Tommy evidently liked it, and stretched out his trunk for a second morsel. But the German was cunning. Holding the tart in his hand he went up the staircase, step by step, and the elephant unwillingly followed him with outstretched trunk and bristling ears. On the landing Tommy was given a second piece.

In this way they brought him into the dining-room, from whence all the furniture had been taken out beforehand, and the floor had been strewn with a thick layer of straw. . . . Tommy was fastened by the leg to a ring which had been screwed into the floor. They put some fresh carrots, cabbages and turnips in front of him. The German stretched himself out on a sofa by Tommy's side. The lights were put out, and everybody went to bed.

VI

Next morning the little girl woke very early, and asked, first thing :

" The elephant ? Has he come ? "

" Yes, he's come," said mamma; " but he says that Nadya must first of all be washed, and then eat a soft-boiled egg and drink some hot milk."

" Is he good ? "

" Yes, he's good. Eat it up, dear. We'll go and see him in a minute."

" Is he funny ? "

" Yes, a little.   Put on your warm bodice."

The egg was quickly eaten, and the milk drunk. Nadya was put in the perambulator in which she used to be taken out when she was too small to walk by herself, and wheeled into the dining-room.

The elephant looked much larger than Nadya had thought when she saw it in a picture.   He was only just a little lower than the top of the door, and half as long as the dining-room.   He had thick skin, in heavy folds.   His legs were thick as pillars.   His long tail looked something like a broom at the end.   His head had great lumps on it.   His ears were as large as shovels, and were hanging down.   His eyes were quite tiny, but they looked wise and kind.   His tusks had been cut off.   His trunk was like a long snake and had two nostrils at the end, with a moving flexible finger between them.   If the elephant had stretched out his trunk to its full length, it would probably have reached to the window.

The little girl was not at all frightened.   She was only just a little astounded by the enormous size of the animal.   But Polya, the sixteen-year-old nursemaid, began to whimper in terror.

The elephant's master, the German, came up to the perambulator and said :

" Good morning, young lady.   Don't be afraid, please.   Tommy's very good, and he likes children."

The little girl held out her little white hand to the German.

" Good morning," she said in answer.   " How are you ? I'm not in the least afraid.   What's his name ? "

" Tommy."

" Good morning, Tommy," said the child, with a bow. " How did you sleep last night ? "

She held out her hand to him. The elephant took it cautiously and pressed her thin fingers with his movable strong one, and he did this much more gently than Dr. Michael Petrovitch. Then he nodded his head, and screwed up his little eyes as if he were laughing.

" Does he understand everything ? " asked the little girl of the German.

" Oh, absolutely everything, miss."

" Only he can't speak."

" No, he can't speak. Do you know, I've got a little girl just as small as you. Her name's Lisa. Tommy's a great, a very great, friend of hers."

" And you, Tommy, have you had any tea yet ? " asked Nadya.

The elephant stretched out his trunk and blew out a warm breath into the little girl's face, making her hair puff out at each side.

Nadya laughed and clapped her hands. The German laughed out loud too. He was also large and fat, and good-natured like the elephant, and Nadya thought they looked like one another. Perhaps they were relations.

" No, he hasn't had tea, miss. But he likes to drink sugar-water. And he's very fond of rolls."

Some rolls were brought in on a tray. The little girl handed some to her guest. He caught a roll cleverly with his finger, and turning up his trunk into a ring hid the roll somewhere underneath his head, where one could see his funny three-cornered, hairy, lower lip moving, and hear the roll rustling against the dry skin. Tommy did the same with a second roll, and a third, and a fourth and a fifth, nodding his head and wrinkling up his little eyes still more with satisfaction. And the little girl laughed delightedly.

When the rolls were all eaten, Nadya presented her dolls to the elephant.

" Look, Tommy, this nicely-dressed doll is Sonya. She's a very good child, but a little naughty sometimes, and doesn't want to eat her soup. This one is Natasha, Sonya's daughter. She's begun to learn already, and she knows almost all her letters. And this one is Matreshka. She was my very first doll. Look, she hasn't got any nose and her head's been stuck on, and she's lost all her hair. But I can't turn an old woman out of the house. Can I, Tommy ? She used to be Sonya's mother, but now she's the cook. Let's have a game, Tommy ; you be the father and I'll be the mother, and these shall be our children."

Tommy agreed. He laughed, took Matreshka by the neck and put her in his mouth. But this was only a joke. After biting the doll a little he put her back again on the little girl's lap, just a little wet and crumpled.

Then Nadya showed him a large picture-book, and explained :

" This is a horse, this is a canary, this is a gun. . . . Look, there's a cage with a bird inside ; here's a pail, a looking-glass, a stove, a spade, a raven. . . . And here, just look, here's an elephant. It's not at all like you, is it ? Is it possible an elephant could be so small, Tommy ? "

Tommy thought that there were no elephants in the world as small as that. He didn't seem to like that picture. He took hold of the edge of the page with his finger and turned it over.

It was dinner-time now, but the little girl couldn't tear herself away from the elephant. The German came to the rescue.

" If you allow me, I will arrange it all. They can dine together."

He ordered the elephant to sit down, and the obedient animal did so, shaking all the floor of the whole flat, making all the china on the sideboard jingle, and the people downstairs were sprinkled over with bits of plaster falling from the ceiling. The little girl sat opposite the elephant. The table was put between them. A tablecloth was tied round the elephant's neck, and the new friends began their dinner. The little girl had chicken broth and cutlets, the elephant had various vegetables and salad. The little girl had a liqueur glass full of sherry, and the elephant had some warm water with a glassful of rum in it, and he sucked up this liquid through his trunk with great pleasure from a soup tureen. Then they had the sweet course—the little girl a cup of cocoa, and the elephant a tart, a walnut one this time. The German, meanwhile, sat with papa in the drawing-room, and, with as much pleasure as the elephant, drank beer, only in greater quantities.

After dinner some visitors came to see papa, and they were warned in the hall about the elephant so that they should not be frightened. At first they couldn't believe it, but when they saw Tommy they pressed themselves close up against the door.

" Don't be afraid, he's good," said the little girl soothingly.

But the visitors quickly hurried into the drawing-room, and after having sat there for five minutes took their departure.

The evening came. It grew late, and time for the little girl to go to bed. But they couldn't get her away from the elephant. She dropped asleep by his side presently, and then they carried her off to the nursery. She didn't wake up, even when she was being undressed.

That night Nadya dreamed that she was married to Tommy and that they had many children, tiny, jolly, little baby elephants. The elephant, whom they took back at night to the menagerie, also dreamed of the sweet and affectionate little girl. He dreamt, too, that he had a large tart with walnuts and pistachios as big as a gate. . . .

Next morning the little girl woke, fresh and healthy, and as she used to do before her illness, cried out, in a voice to be heard all over the house, loudly and impatiently :

" I want some milk."

Hearing this cry, in her bedroom mamma crossed herself devoutly.

But the little girl remembered what had happened yesterday, and she asked :

" Where's the elephant ? "

They explained to her that the elephant had been obliged to go home, that he had children who couldn't be left by themselves, but that he had left a message for Nadya to say that he hoped she would come and see him as soon as she was well.

The little girl smiled slyly and said :

" Tell Tommy that I'm quite well now."

N

XI

DOGS' HAPPINESS

IT was between six and seven o'clock on a fine September morning when the eighteen-months-old pointer, Jack, a brown, long-eared, frisky animal, started out with the cook, Annushka, to market. He knew the way perfectly well, and so ran confidently on in front of her, sniffing at the curbstones as he went and stopping at the crossings to see if Annushka were following. Finding affirmation in her face, and the direction in which she was going, he would turn again with a decisive movement and rush on in a lively gallop.

On one occasion, however, when he turned round near a familiar sausage-shop, Jack could not see Annushka. He dashed back so hastily that his left ear was turned inside out as he went. But Annushka was not to be seen at the cross-roads. So Jack resolved to find his way by scent. He stopped, cautiously raised his wet sensitive nose, and tried in all directions to recognise the familiar scent of Annushka's dress, the smell of the dirty kitchen-table and mottled soap. But just at that moment a lady came hurriedly past him, and brushing up against his side with her rustling skirt she left behind a strong wave of disgusting Oriental perfume. Jack moved his head from side to side in vexation. The trail of Annushka was entirely lost.

But he was not upset by this. He knew the town well and could always find his way home easily—all he had to do was to go to the sausage-shop, then to the greengrocer's, then turn to the left and go past a grey house from the basement of which there was always wafted a smell of burning fat, and he would be in his own street. Jack did not hurry. The morning was fresh and clear, and in the pure, softly transparent and rather moist air, all the various odours of the town had an unusual refinement and distinctness. Running past the post-office, with his tail stuck out as stiff as a rod and his nostrils all trembling with excitement, Jack could have sworn that only a moment before a large, mouse-coloured, oldish dog had stopped there, a dog who was usually fed on oatmeal porridge.

And after running along about two hundred paces, he actually saw this dog, a cowardly, sober-looking brute. His ears had been cropped, and a broad, worn, strap was dangling from his neck.

The dog noticed Jack, and stopped, half turning back on his steps. Jack curled his tail in the air provokingly and began to walk slowly round the other, with an air of looking somewhere to one side. The mouse-coloured dog also raised his tail and showed a broad row of white teeth. Then they both growled, turning their heads away from one another as they did so, and trying, as it were, to swallow something which stuck in their throats.

" If he says anything insulting to my honour, or the honour of any well-bred pointer, I shall fasten my teeth in his side, near his left hind-leg," thought Jack to himself. " Of course, he is stronger than I am, but he is stupid and clumsy. Look how he stands there, like a dummy, and has no idea that all his left flank is open to attack.''

And suddenly . . . something inexplicable and almost supernatural happened. The other dog unexpectedly threw himself on his back and was dragged by some unseen force from the pathway into the road. Directly afterwards this same unseen power grasped Jack by the throat . . . he stood firm on his fore-legs and shook his head furiously. But the invisible '' something '' was pulled so tight round his neck that the brown pointer became unconscious.[1]

He came to his senses again in a stuffy iron cage, which was jolting and shaking as it was drawn along the cobbled roadway, on a badly-jointed vehicle trembling in all its parts. From its acrid doggy odour Jack guessed at once that this cart must have been used for years to convey dogs of all breeds and all ages. On the box in front sat two men, whose outward appearance was not at all calculated to inspire confidence.

There was already a sufficiently large company in the cart. First of all, Jack noticed the mouse-coloured dog whom he had just met and quarrelled with in the street. He was standing with his head stuck out between two of the iron bars, and he whined pitifully as his body was jolted backwards and forwards by the movement of the cart. In the middle of the cage lay an old white poodle, his wise-looking head lying between his gouty paws. His coat was cut to make him look like a lion, with tufts left on his knees

---

[1] Some municipalities in Russia provide a man and a cart to take off stray dogs. Jack had been suddenly netted by the dog-man.

and at the end of his tail.   The poodle had apparently
resigned himself to his situation with a stoic philosophy,
and if he had not sighed occasionally and wrinkled
his brows, it might have been thought that he slept.
By his side, trembling from agitation and the cold
of the early morning, sat a fine well-kept greyhound,
with long thin legs and sharp-pointed head.   She
yawned nervously from time to time, rolling up her
rosy little tongue into a tube, accompanying the yawn
with a long-drawn-out, high-pitched whine. . . . Near
the back of the cage, pressed close up to the bars,
was a black dachshund, with smooth skin dappled
with yellow on the breast and above the eyes.   She
could not get over her astonishment at her position,
and she looked a strangely comical figure with her
flopping paws and crocodile body, and the serious
expression of her head with its ears reaching almost
to the ground.

Besides this more or less distinguished society,
there were in the cage two unmistakable yard dogs.
One of them was that sort of dog which is generally
called Bouton, and is always noted for its meanness
of disposition.   She was a shaggy, reddish-coloured
animal with a shaggy tail, curled up like the figure 9.
She had been the first of the dogs to be captured,
and she had apparently become so accustomed to
her position that she had for some time past made
many efforts to begin an interesting conversation
with someone.   The last dog of all was out of sight,
he had been driven into the darkest corner, and lay
there curled up in a heap.   He had only moved once
all the time, and that had been to growl at Jack
when he had found himself near him.   Everyone in

the company felt a strong antipathy against him. In the first place, he was smeared all over with a violet colour, the work of certain journeyman whitewashers; secondly, his hair was rough and bristly and uncombed; thirdly, he was evidently mangy, hungry, strong and daring—this had been quite evident in the resolute push of his lean body with which he had greeted the arrival of the unconscious Jack.

There was silence for a quarter of an hour. At last Jack, whose healthy sense of humour never forsook him under any circumstances, remarked in a jaunty tone :

" The adventure begins to be interesting. I am curious to know where these gentlemen will make their first stopping place."

The old poodle did not like the frivolous tone of the brown pointer. He turned his head slowly in Jack's direction, and said sharply, with a cold sarcasm :

" I can satisfy your curiosity, young man. These gentlemen will make their first stopping place at the slaughter-house."

" Where ? Pardon me, please, I didn't catch the word," muttered Jack, sitting down involuntarily, for his legs had suddenly begun to tremble. " You were pleased to say—at the s-s . . ."

" Yes, at the slaughter-house," repeated the poodle coldly, turning his head away.

" Pardon me, but I don't quite understand. . . . Slaughter-house ? . . . What kind of an institution is that ? Won't you be so good as to explain ? "

The poodle was silent. But as the greyhound and the terrier both joined their petition to Jack's, the old poodle, who did not wish to appear impolite in the presence of ladies, felt obliged to enter into certain details.

"Well, you see *mesdames*, it is a sort of large court-yard surrounded by a high fence with sharp points, where they shut in all dogs found wandering in the streets. I've had the unhappiness to bé taken there three times already."

"I've never seen you!" was heard in a hoarse voice from the dark corner. "And this is the seventh time I've been there."

There was no doubt that the voice from the dark corner belonged to the violet-coloured dog. The company was shocked at the interruption of their conversation by this rude person, and so pretended not to hear the remark. But Bouton, with the cringing eagerness of an upstart in society, cried out : "Please don't interfere in other people's conversation unless you're asked," and then turned at once to the important-looking mouse-coloured dog for approbation.

"I've been there three times," the poodle went on, "but my master has always come and fetched me away again. I play in a circus, and you understand that I am of some value. Well, in this unpleasant place they have a collection of two or three hundred dogs. . . ."

"But, tell me . . . is there good society there?" asked the greyhound affectedly.

"Sometimes. They feed us very badly and give us little to eat. Occasionally one of the dogs disappears, and then they give us a dinner of . . ."

In order to heighten the effect of his words, the poodle made a slight pause, looked round on his audience, and then added with studied indifference :

—" Of dog's flesh."

At these words the company was filled with terror and indignation.

" Devil take it . . . what low-down scoundrelism ! " exclaimed Jack.

" I shall faint . . . I feel so ill," murmured the greyhound.

" That's dreadful . . . dreadful . . ." moaned the dachshund.

" I've always said that men were scoundrels," snarled the mouse-coloured dog.

" What a strange death ! " sighed Bouton.

But from the dark corner was heard once more the voice of the violet-coloured dog. With gloomy and cynical sarcasm he said :

" The soup's not so bad, though—it's not at all bad, though, of course, some ladies who are accustomed to eat chicken cutlets would find dog's flesh a little too tough."

The poodle paid no attention to this rude remark, but went on :

" And afterwards I gathered from the manager's talk that our late companion's skin had gone to make ladies' gloves. But . . . prepare your nerves, *mesdames* . . . but, this is nothing. . . . In order to make the skin softer and more smooth, it must be taken from the living animal."

Cries of despair broke in upon the poodle's speech.

" How inhuman ! "

" What mean conduct ! "

" No, that can't be true ! "

" O Lord ! "

" Murderers ! "

" No, worse than murderers ! "

After this outburst there was a strained and melancholy silence. Each of them had a mental picture, a fearful foreboding of what it might be to be skinned alive.

" Ladies and gentlemen, is there no way of getting all honourable dogs free, once and for all, from their shameful slavery to mankind ? " cried Jack passionately.

" Be so good as to find a way," said the old poodle ironically.

The dogs all began to try and think of a way.

" Bite them all, and have an end of it ! " said the big dog in his angry bass.

" Yes, that's the way ; we need a radical remedy," seconded the servile Bouton. " In the end they'll be afraid of us."

" Yes, bite them all—that's a splendid idea," said the old poodle. " But what's your opinion, dear sirs, about their long whips ? No doubt you're acquainted with them ! "

" H'm." The dog coughed and cleared his throat.

" H'm," echoed Bouton.

" No, take my word for it, gentlemen, we cannot struggle against men. I've lived in this world for some time, and I've not had a bad life. . . . Take for example such simple things as kennels, whips, chains, muzzles—things, I imagine, not unknown to any one of us. Let us suppose that we dogs succeed in thinking out a plan which will free us from these things. Will not man then arm himself with more perfect instruments ? There is no doubt that he will. Haven't you seen what instruments of torture they make for one another ? No, we must submit to them, gentlemen, that's all about it. It's a law of Nature."

" Well, he's shown us his philosophy," whispered the dachshund in Jack's ear. " I've no patience with these old folks and their teaching."

" You're quite right, *mademoiselle*," said Jack, gallantly wagging his tail.

The mouse-coloured dog was looking very melancholy and snapping at the flies. He drawled out in a whining tone :

" Eh, it's a dog's life ! "

" And where is the justice of it all ? "—the greyhound, who had been silent up to this point, began to agitate herself—" You, Mr. Poodle, pardon me, I haven't the honour of knowing your name."

" Arto, professor of equilibristics, at your service." The poodle bowed.

" Well, tell me, Mr. Professor, you have apparently had such great experience, let alone your learning— tell me, where is the higher justice of it all ? Are human beings so much more worthy and better than we are, that they are allowed to take advantage of so many cruel privileges with impunity ? "

" They are not any better or any more worthy than we are, dear young lady, but they are stronger and wiser," answered Arto, with some heat. " Oh, I know the morals of these two-legged animals very well. . . . In the first place, they are greedy—greedier than any dog on earth. They have so much bread and meat and water that all these monsters could be satisfied and well-fed all their lives. But instead of sharing it out, a tenth of them get all the provisions for life into their hands, and not being able to devour it all themselves, they force the remaining nine-tenths to go hungry. Now, tell me, is it possible that a well-fed dog would not share a gnawed bone with his neighbour ? "

" He'd share it, of course he would ! " agreed all the listeners.

" H'm," coughed the dog doubtfully.

" And besides that, people are wicked. Who could ever say that one dog would kill another—on account of love or envy or malice ? We bite one another sometimes, that's true. But we don't take each other's lives."

" No, indeed we don't," they all affirmed.

" And more than this," went on the white poodle. " Could one dog make up his mind not to allow another dog to breathe the fresh air, or to be free to express his thoughts as to the arrangements for the happiness of dogs ? But men do this."

" Devil take them ! " put in the mouse-coloured dog energetically.

" And, in conclusion, I say that men are hypocrites ; they envy one another, they lie, they are inhospitable, cruel. . . . And yet they rule over us, and will continue to do so . . . because it's arranged like that. It is impossible for us to free ourselves from their authority. All the life of dogs, and all their happiness, is in the hands of men. In our present position each one of us, who has a good master, ought to thank Fate. Only a master can free us from the pleasure of eating a comrade's flesh, and of imagining that comrade's feelings when he was being skinned alive."

The professor's speech reduced the whole company to a state of melancholy. No other dog could utter a word. They all shivered helplessly, and shook with the joltings of the cart. The big dog whined piteously. Bouton, who was standing next to him, pressed his own body softly up against him.

But soon they felt that the wheels of the cart were passing over sand. In five minutes more they were driven through wide open gates, and they found themselves in the middle of an immense courtyard surrounded by a close paling. Sharp nails were sticking out at the top of the paling. Two hundred dogs, lean and dirty, with drooping tails and a look of melancholy on their faces, wandered about the yard.

The doors of the cage were flung open. All the seven new-comers came forth and instinctively stood together in one group.

" Here, you professor, how do you feel now ? " The poodle heard a bark behind him.

He turned round and saw the violet-coloured dog smiling insolently at him.

" Oh, leave me alone," growled the old poodle. " It's no business of yours."

" I only made a remark," said the other. " You spoke such words of wisdom in the cart, but you made one mistake. Yes, you did."

" Get away, devil take you ! What mistake ? "

" About a dog's happiness. If you like, I'll show you in whose hands a dog's happiness lies."

And suddenly pressing back his ears and extending his tail, the violet dog set out on such a mad career that the old professor of equilibristics could only stand and watch him with open mouth.

" Catch him ! Stop him ! " shouted the keepers, flinging themselves in pursuit of the escaping dog.

But the violet dog had already gained the paling. With one bound he sprang up from the ground and found himself at the top, hanging on by his fore-paws. And in two more convulsive springs he had leaped over the paling, leaving on the nails a good half of his side.

The old white poodle gazed after him for a long time. He understood the mistake he had made.

XII

A CLUMP OF LILACS

Nikolai Yevgrafovitch Almazof hardly waited
for his wife to open the door to him ; he went straight
to his study without taking off his hat or coat. His
wife knew in a moment by his frowning face and
nervously-bitten underlip that a great misfortune
had occurred.

She followed him in silence. Almazof stood still
for a moment when he reached the study, and stared
gloomily into one corner, then he dashed his portfolio
out of his hand on to the floor, where it lay wide open,
and threw himself into an armchair, irritably snapping
his fingers together.

He was a young and poor army officer attending
a course of lectures at the staff office academy, and
had just returned from a class. To-day he had taken
in to the professor his last and most difficult practical
work, a survey of the neighbourhood.

So far all his examinations had gone well, and it
was only known to God and to his wife what fearful
labour they had cost him. . . . To begin with, his very
entrance into the academy had seemed impossible
at first. Two years in succession he had failed
ignominiously, and only in the third had he by determined effort overcome all hindrances. If it hadn't
been for his wife he would not have had sufficient

energy to continue the struggle ; he would have given it up entirely. But Verotchka never allowed him to lose heart, she was always encouraging him . . . she met every drawback with a bright, almost gay, front. She denied herself everything so that her husband might have all the little things so necessary for a man engaged in mental labour ; she was his secretary, draughtsman, reader, lesson-hearer, and note-book all in one.

For five minutes there was a dead silence, broken only by the sorry sound of their old alarm clock, familiar and tiresome . . . one, two, three-three— two clear ticks, and the third with a hoarse stammer. Almazof still sat in his hat and coat, turning to one side in his chair. . . . Vera stood two paces from him, silent also, her beautiful mobile face full of suffering. At length she broke the stillness with the cautiousness a woman might use when speaking at the bedside of a very sick friend :

" Well, Kolya, what about the work ?   Was it bad ? "

He shrugged his shoulders without speaking.

" Kolya, was it rejected ?   Tell me ; we must talk it over together."

Almazof turned to his wife and began to speak irritably and passionately, as one generally does speak when telling of an insult long endured.

" Yes, yes. They've rejected it, if you want to know. Can't you see they have ?   It's all gone to the devil !   All that rubbish "—he kicked the portfolio with his foot—" all that rubbish had better be thrown into the fire. That's your academy. I shall be back in the regiment with a bang next month, disgraced. And all for a filthy spot . . . damn it ! "

" What spot, Kolya ? " asked she. " I don't understand anything about it."

She sat down on the side of his chair and put her arm round his neck. He made no resistance, but still continued to stare into the corner with an injured expression.

" What spot was it, Kolya ? " asked his wife once more.

" Oh, an ordinary spot—of green paint. You know I sat up until three o'clock last night to finish my drawing. The plan was beautifully done. Everyone said so. Well, I sat there last night and I got so tired that my hand shook, and I made a blot—such a big one. . . . I tried to erase it, but I only made it worse. . . . I thought and thought what I had better do, and I made up my mind to put a clump of trees in that place. . . . It was very successful, and no one could guess there had been a blot. Well, to-day I took it in to the professor. ' Yes, yes,' said he, ' that's very well. But what have you got here, lieutenant ; where have these bushes sprung from ? ' Of course, I ought to have told him what had happened. Perhaps he would only have laughed . . . but no, he wouldn't, he's such an accurate German, such a pedant. So I said, ' There are some trees growing there.' ' Oh, no, no,' said he. ' I know this neighbourhood as well as I know the five fingers of my own hand ; there can't be any trees there.' So, my word against his, we had a great argument about it ; many of our officers were there too, listening. ' Well,' he said at last, ' if you're so sure that there are trees in this hollow, be so good as to ride over with me to-morrow and see. I'll prove to you that you've either done your work carelessly, or that you've copied it from a three versts to the inch map. . . .' "

" But why was he so certain that no bushes were there ? "

" Oh, Lord, why ? What childish questions you do ask ! Because he's known this district for twenty years ; he knows it better than his own bedroom. He's the most fearful pedant in the world, and a German besides. . . . Well, of course, he'll know in the end that I was lying and so discussed the point with him. . . ."

All the time he spoke he kept picking up burnt matches from the ash-tray on the table in front of him, and breaking them to little bits. When he ceased speaking, he threw the pieces on the floor. It was quite evident that, strong man though he was, he was very near weeping.

For a long while husband and wife sat there silent. Then suddenly Verotchka jumped up from her seat.

" Listen, Kolya," said she. " We must go this very minute. Make haste and get ready."

Nikolai Yevgrafovitch wrinkled up his face as if he were suffering some intolerable pain.

" Oh, don't talk nonsense, Vera," he said. " You don't think I can go and put matters right by apologising, do you ? That would be asking for punishment. Don't be foolish, please ! "

" No, it's not foolishness," said Vera, stamping her foot. " Nobody wants you to go and apologise. But, don't you see, if there aren't any silly old trees there we'd better go and put some."

" Put some—trees ! " exclaimed Nikolai Yevgrafovitch, his eyes staring.

" Yes, put some there. If you didn't speak the truth, then you must make it true. Come along, get ready. Give me my hat . . . and coat. No, not there ; in the cupboard. . . . Umbrella ! "

And while Almazof, finding his objections entirely ignored, began to look for the hat and coat, Vera opened drawers and brought out various little boxes and cases.

" Earrings. . . . No, they're no good. We shan't get anything on them. Ah, here's this ring with the valuable stone. We'll have to buy that back some time. It would be a pity to lose it. Bracelet . . . they won't give much for that either, it's old and bent. . . . Where's your silver cigar-case, Kolya ? "

In five minutes all their valuables were in her handbag, and Vera, dressed and ready, looked round for the last time to assure herself she hadn't overlooked anything.

" Let us go," she said at last, resolutely.

" But where ? " Almazof tried again to protest. " It's beginning to get dark already, and the place is ten versts away."

" Stupid ! Come along."

First of all they went to the pawnshop. The pawnbroker had evidently got accustomed long ago to the sight of people in distress, and could not be touched by it. He was so methodical about his work, and took so long to value the things, that Vera felt she should go crazy. What specially vexed her was that the man should test her ring with acid, and then, after weighing it, he valued it at three roubles only.

" But it's a real brilliant," said poor Vera. " It

cost thirty - seven roubles, and then it was a bargain."

The pawnbroker closed his eyes with the air of a man who is frankly bored.

"It's all the same to us, madam," said he, putting the next article into the scales. "We don't take the stones into consideration, only the metals."

To Vera's astonishment, her old and bent bracelet was more valuable. Altogether they got about twenty-three roubles, and that was more than was really necessary.

When they got to the gardener's house, the white Petersburg night had already spread over the heavens, and a pearly light was in the air. The gardener, a Tchekh, a little old man with gold eyeglasses, had only just sat down to supper with his family. He was much surprised at their request, and not altogether willing to take such a late order. He was doubtless suspicious of a practical joke, and answered dryly to Vera's insistent demands :

"I'm very sorry. But I can't send my workmen so far at night. If it will do to-morrow morning, I'm quite at your service."

There was no way out of the difficulty but to tell the man the whole story of the unfortunate blot, and this Verotchka did. He listened doubtfully at first, and was almost unfriendly, but when Vera began to tell him of her plan to plant some bushes on the place, he became more attentive and smiled sympathetically several times.

"Oh, well, it's not much to do," he agreed, when Vera had finished her story. "What sort of bushes do you want ? "

However, when they came to look at his plants, there was nothing very suitable. The only thing possible to put on the spot was a clump of lilacs.

It was in vain for Almazof to try and persuade his wife to go home. She went all the way with him, and stayed all the time the bushes were planted, feverishly fussing about and hindering the workmen. She only consented to go home when she was assured that the turf under the bushes could not be distinguished from the rest of the grass round about.

Next day Vera felt it impossible to remain in the house. She went out to meet her husband. Quite a long way off she knew, by a slight spring in his walk, that everything had gone well. . . . True, Almazof was covered in dust, and he could hardly move from weariness and hunger, but his face shone with the triumph of victory.

" It's all right ! Splendid ! " cried he when within ten paces of his wife, in answer to the anxious expression on her face. " Just think, we went together to those bushes, and he looked and looked at them—he even plucked a leaf and chewed it. ' What sort of a tree is this ? ' says he."

" ' I don't know, your Excellency,' said I.

" ' It's a little birch, I suppose,' says he.

" ' Yes, probably, your Excellency.' "

Then he turned to me and held out his hand.

" ' I beg your pardon, lieutenant,' he says. ' I must be getting old, that I didn't remember those bushes.' He's a fine man, that professor, and he knows a lot. I felt quite sorry to deceive him. He's one of the best professors we have. His learning is simply wonderful. And how quick and accurate he is in marking the plans—marvellous ! ”

But this meant little to Vera. She wanted to hear over and over again exactly what the professor had said about the bushes. She was interested in the smallest details—the expression on the professor's face, the tone of his voice when he said he must be growing old, exactly how Kolya felt . . .

They went home together as if there had been no one in the street except themselves, holding each other by the hand and laughing at nothing. The passers-by stopped to look at them ; they seemed such a strange couple.

Never before had Nikolai Yevgrafovitch enjoyed his dinner so much as on that day. After dinner, when Vera brought a glass of tea to him in the study, husband and wife suddenly looked at one another, and both laughed.

“ What are you laughing at ? ” asked Vera.

“ Well, why did *you* laugh ? ” said her husband.

“ Oh, only foolishness. I was thinking all about those lilacs. And you ? ”

“ Oh, mine was foolishness too—and the lilacs. I was just going to say that now the lilac will always be my favourite flower. . . .”

XIII

ANATHEMA

" FATHER DEACON, you're wasting the candles," said the deacon's wife. " It's time to get up."

This small, thin, yellow-faced woman treated her husband very harshly. In the school at which she had been educated there had been an opinion that men were scoundrels, deceivers, and tyrants. But her husband, the deacon, was certainly not a tyrant. He was absolutely in awe of his half-hysterical, half-epileptic, childless wife. The deacon weighed about nine and a half poods [1] of solid flesh ; he had a broad chest like the body of a motor-car, an awful voice, and with it all that gentle condescension of manner which often marks the behaviour of extraordinarily strong people in their relations towards the weak.

It always took the deacon a long time to get his voice in order. This occupation—an unpleasant, long-drawn-out torture—is, of course, well known to all those who have to sing in public : the rubbing with cocaine, the burning with caustic, the gargling with boracic acid. And, still lying upon his bed, Father Olympus began to try his voice.

" Via . . . kmm ! Via-a-a ! Alleluia, alleluia. . . . Oba-che . . . kmm. . . . Ma-ma. . . ."

[1] A pood is 40 Russian lbs., about 36 lbs. English.

" There's no sound in my voice," he said to himself. " Vla-di-ko bla-go-slo-ve-e-e. . . . Km. . . ."

Like all famous singers, he was given to be anxious about his voice. It is well known that actors grow pale and cross themselves before they go on to the stage. And Father Olympus suffered from this vice of fear. Yet he was the only man in the town, and possibly in all Russia, who could make his voice resound in the old dark cathedral church, gleaming with ancient gold and mosaic.

He alone could fill all the corners of the old building with his powerful voice, and when he intoned the funeral service every crystal lustre in the candelabras trembled and jingled with the sound.

His prim wife brought him in a glass of weak tea with lemon in it, and, as usual on Sunday mornings, a glass of vodka. Olympus tried his voice once more: " Mi . . . mi . . . fa. . . . Mi-ro-no-citsi. . . . Here, mother," called he to his wife, " give me *re* on the harmonium."

His wife sounded a long melancholy note.

" Km . . . km. . . . Pharaoh and his chariots. . . . No, no, I can't do it, my voice has gone. The devil must have got into me from that writer, what's his name ? . . ."

Father Olympus was very fond of reading ; he read much and indiscriminately, but paid very little attention to the names of the authors. His seminary education, based chiefly on learning by heart, on reading " rubrics," on learning indispensable quotations from the fathers of the Church, had developed his memory to an unusual degree. In order to get by heart a whole page of complicated casuistical reasoning.

such as that of St. Augustine, Tertullian, Origen, Basil the Great or St. John Chrysostom, it was quite sufficient for him to run his eye over the lines, and he would remember them. It was a student from the Bethany Academy who brought him books to read, and only the evening before he had given him a delightful romance, a picture of life in the Caucasus, of soldiers, Cossacks, Tchetchenians, and how they lived there and fought one another, drank wine, married, hunted.

The reading of this tale had disturbed the elementary soul of the deacon. He had read it three times over, and often during the reading had laughed and wept emotionally, clenching his fists and turning his huge body from one side to the other in his chair. He continually asked himself, " Would it not have been better to have been a hunter, a trapper, a fisherman, a horseman, anything rather than a clergyman? "

* * * * *

He was always a little later in coming into the cathedral than he ought to have been. Just like a famous baritone at a theatre. As he came through the south door into the sanctuary, on this Sunday morning, he tried his voice for the last time. " Km . . . km. . . . I can sing *re*," he thought. " But that scoundrel will certainly give me the tone on *doh*. Never mind, I must change it to my note, and the choir will be obliged to follow."

There awoke in him that pride which always slumbers in the breast of a public favourite, for he was spoilt by the whole town ; even the street-boys used to collect together to stare at him with a similar veneration to that with which they gazed into the

immense mouth of the brass helicon in the military
band on the boulevard.

The bishop entered and was solemnly installed in
his seat. He wore his mitre a little on one side.
Two sub-deacons stood beside him with censers,
swinging them harmoniously. The clergy, in bright
festival robes, stood around. Two priests brought
forward from the altar the ikons of the Saviour and
the Virgin-Mother, and placed them on a stand before
the people.

The cathedral was an ancient building, and had a
pulpit of carved oak like that of a Catholic church.
It stood close up to the wall, and was reached by a
winding staircase. This was the deacon's place.

Slowly, trying each step as he went, and carefully
resting his hands on the balustrade—he was always
afraid of breaking something accidentally—the deacon
went up into the pulpit. Then, clearing his throat
and nose and expectorating, he struck the tuning-
fork, passed deliberately from *doh* to *re*, and began :

" Bless us, most reverend Father."

" Now, you scoundrel," he thought to himself,
apostrophising the leader of the choir; " you won't
dare to change the tone in the presence of the bishop."
At that moment he felt, with pleasure, that his voice
sounded much better than usual ; it was quite easy
to pass from one note to another, and its soft depth
of tone caused all the air in the cathedral to vibrate.

It was the Orthodox service for the first week in
Lent, and, at first, Father Olympus had not much
work. The reader trumpeted out the psalms in-
distinctly ; he was a deacon from the academy, a
future professor of homiletics, and he snuffled.

Father Olympus roared out from time to time, "Let us pray." He stood there on his raised platform, immense, in his stiff vestment of gilt brocade, his mane of grey-black hair hanging on his shoulders, and every now and then he tried his voice quietly. The church was full to the doors with sentimental old peasant women and sturdy grey-bearded peasants.

"Strange," thought Olympus to himself suddenly, "but every one of these women's heads, if I look at it from the side, reminds me inevitably either of the head of a fish or of a hen's head. Even the deaconess, my wife. . . ."

His attention, however, was not diverted from the service. He followed it all along in his seventeenth-century missal. The prayers came to an end: "Almighty God, Master and Creator of all living." And at last, "Amen."

Then began the affirmation of Orthodoxy. "Who is as great as the Lord, as our God? Thou art the God who alone doest wonders." The chant had many turns in it, and was not particularly clear. Generally during the first week in Lent there follows, at this point, the ritual of anathema, which can be altered or omitted as may be thought fit by the bishop. There is a list of persons to be anathematised for special reasons, Mazeppa is cursed, Stenka Razin, Arius the iconoclast, the old-believer Avvakum, etc., etc.

But the deacon was not quite himself to-day. Certainly he must have been a little upset by the vodka his wife had given him that morning. For some reason or other he could not get the story which he had read the previous night out of his mind. He kept seeing clear and vivid pictures of a beautiful, simple, and boundlessly attractive life. Almost mechanically he went through the Creed, chanted the Amen, and proclaimed according to an ancient custom to an old and solemn tone : " This is the faith of the apostles, this is the faith of our fathers, this is the Orthodox faith, this is the universal faith, this faith is ours."

The archbishop was a great formalist, a pedant, and a somewhat eccentric man. He never allowed a word to be dropped out of the text of the canon of our thrice-blessed Father Andrew of Crete, or from the funeral service or from any other rite. And Father Olympus, imperturbably causing the cathedral to vibrate with his lion's roar, and making the lustres of the candelabra jingle and sound as they moved, cursed, anathematised and excommunicated from the Church the iconoclasts, all the ancient heretics from Arius onward, all those accepting the teaching of Ital, of the monk Nil, of Constantine Bulgaris and Irinik, of Varlaam and Akindin, of Gerontius and Isaac Agrir ; cursed those who insulted the Church, all Mahometans, Dissenters and Judaizers ; cursed the reproachers of the festival of the Annunciation, smugglers, offenders of widows and orphans, the Old-Believers, the rebels and traitors, Grishka, Otrepief, Timoshka Akundinof, Stenka Razin, Ivashka Mazeppa, Emelka Pugachof, as well as all those who uphold any teaching contrary to that of the Orthodox faith.

Then the extent of the curse was proclaimed : denial of the blessings of redemption, exclusion from the Holy Sacraments, and expulsion from the assembly of the holy fathers and their inheritance.

Curses were pronounced on those who do not think that the Orthodox Tsar was raised to the throne by the special will of God, when at his anointing, at the commencement of his high calling, the holy oil was poured out upon him ; also on those daring to stir up sedition against him ; on those who abuse and blaspheme the holy ikons. And to each of these proclamations the choir responded in a mournful wail, tender angelic voices giving the response, " *Anathema.*"

The women had long been weeping hysterically.

The deacon was about to end by singing the " Eternal Memory " for all those departed this life in the true faith, when the psalm-singer brought him a little note from the priest, telling him that his Eminence the archbishop had ordered that Count Leo Tolstoy was to be anathematised.

The deacon's throat was sore from much reading. But he cleared his throat by a cough, and began once more : " Bless us, most reverend Father." He guessed, rather than heard, the feeble mutterings of the aged prelate :

" The proto-deacon will now, by the grace of God, pronounce a curse upon a blasphemer and apostate from the faith of Christ, and expel from the Holy Sacraments of the Church Count Leo Tolstoy. In the name of the Father, and of the Son, and of the Holy Ghost."

" Amen," sang the choir.

Father Olympus felt his hair stand on end. It seemed to stick out on all sides, and become stiff and painful as if turning into steel wire. And at that moment his memory recalled with extraordinary clearness the tender words of the story[1] he had read the previous night :

" Rousing himself, Yeroshka raised his head and watched the moths fluttering around the flickering flame of his candle and falling therein.

" ' Fool ! fool ! ' said he to one. ' Whither are you flying ? Fool ! fool ! ' He got up and drove the moths away with his clumsy fingers.

" ' You'll burn yourself, little fool ; come, fly away, there's plenty of room here,' said he, coaxing one of them with gentle voice, and striving to catch hold of it by the wings and send it away. ' You'll destroy yourself, and then I shall be sorry for you.' "

" Good Lord ! Who is it I am to curse ? " said the deacon to himself in terror. " Is it possibly *he*—he who made me feel so much, and weep all last night for joy and rapture ? "

But, obedient to a thousand-year-old custom, he repeated the terribly moving words of cursing and excommunication, and they resounded among the crowd like blows upon a large church bell.

So the curse went on : " The ex-priest Nikita, the monks Sergei, Sabatius—yes, Sabatius—Dorofei, Gabriel—blasphemers, impenitent and stubborn in their heresy—and all who act contrary to the will of God, be they accursed ! . . ."

He waited a moment to take breath. His face was red and perspiring. The arteries on both sides of his throat were swollen, each a finger's thickness. And all the while he proclaimed the curse, Tolstoy's thoughts were in his mind. He remembered another passage :

" Once as I sat beside a stream I saw a little cradle come floating bottom upwards towards me. It was quite whole, only the edges a little broken. And I thought—whose cradle is it ?

[1] Evidently, " The Cossacks," by Tolstoy.—[ED.]

Those devils of soldiers have been to a hamlet and taken away all the stores; one of them must have killed a little child and cut the cradle down from its corner with his knife. How can people do such things? Ah, people have no souls! And at such thoughts I became very sad. I thought—they threw the cradle away and drove out the mother and burned the home, and by and by they'll come to us. . . ."

Still he went on with the curse:

" Those sinning against the Holy Ghost, like Simon the sorcerer and Ananias and Sapphira. As the dog returns to its own vomit again, may their days be few and evil, and may their prayers be turned into sin ; may Satan stand at their right hand ; when they are judged let them be condemned, let their names be blotted out and the memory of them perish from the earth . . . and may the curses and anathemas that fall upon them be manifold. May there come upon them the trembling of Cain, the leprosy of Gehazi, the strangling of Judas, the destruction of Simon the sorcerer, the bursting of Arius, the sudden death of Ananias and Sapphira . . . be they anathema and excommunicate, and unforgiven even in their death ; may their bones be scattered and not buried in the earth ; may they be in eternal torment, and tortured by day and night. . . ."

But Tolstoy had said :

" God has made the world to be a joy to man. There is no sin anywhere, not even in the life of a beast. He lives in one place, lives in another. Where he is there is his home. What God gives he takes. But we say that for such things we shall have to suffer. I think that is all one big falsehood. . . ."

The deacon stopped suddenly, and let his ancient missal fall with a bang. Still more dreadful curses were to come, words which could only have been imagined by the narrow minds of monks in the early centuries of Christianity.

His face had become purple, almost black ; his fingers convulsively grasped the rail of the desk. For a moment he felt that he must swoon. But he recovered, and straining the whole might of his tremendous voice, he burst forth triumphantly with new words, wrong words :

" The joy of our earth, the ornament and the flower of life, the true servant and fellow-soldier of Christ, Count Leo. . . ."

He was silent for a second. In the crowded church there was not a cough, not a whisper nor a shuffle of the foot. There was a terrible silence, the silence of hundreds of people dominated by one will, overcome by one feeling. The eyes of the deacon were burning and brimming over with tears, his face became suddenly beautiful as the face of a man in an ecstasy of inspiration. He cleared his throat once more, tried an octave, and then suddenly filling the enormous cathedral with the tones of his terrible voice, he roared out :

" *Mno-ga-ya lye-e-e-ta-a-a.* Ma-any ye-e-ears." And instead of turning the candle upside down, according to the rite of anathema, he raised it high in the air.

It was in vain that the leader of the choir whispered to his boys to knock the deacon's head with the tuning-fork, or to put their hands over his mouth. Joyfully, as if an archangel were blowing a trumpet with silver tones, the deacon lifted his voice over the whole congregation: " *Mnogaya, mnogaya, mnogaya lyeta.*"

The prior, a monk, an official, the psalm-reader and the deaconess rushed up to him.

"Leave me alone . . . leave me alone," said Father Olympus in an angry whisper, roughly pushing away the monk's arm. " I've spoilt my voice, but it has been for the glory of God. Go away ! . . ."

He took off his brocaded vestment at the altar, kissed his stole with emotion, crossed himself before the altar ikon, and went out of the church. He went out, a whole head taller than the people round him, immense, majestic, solemn. And the people involuntarily made way for him, looking at him with a strange timorousness. His look was adamant as he passed the bishop's chair, and without turning his eyes that way he strode out into the vestibule.

In the open space before the church his little wife caught him up, and weeping and pulling his cassock by the sleeve, she gasped :

" What have you gone and done, idiot, cursed one ! Been guzzling vodka all the morning, disgraceful drunkard ! You'll be in luck's way if you only get sent to a monastery for this, and given a scavenger's job. Booh ! You, Cossack of Cherkask ! How many people's doorsteps shall I have to wear out to get you out of this ? Herod ! Oh, you stupid bungler ! "

" It doesn't matter," whispered the deacon to himself, with his eyes on the ground. " I will go and carry bricks or be a signalman or a sledge driver or a house porter ; but, anyhow, I shall give up my post. Yes, to-morrow—I don't want to go on ; I can't any longer. My soul won't stand it. I firmly believe in the Creed and in Christ, and in the Apostolic Church. But I can't assent to malice. ' God has made the world to be a joy to man,' " he quoted suddenly the beautiful, familiar words.

" You're a .fool, a blockhead," cried his wife. " I'll have to put you in an asylum. I'll go to the governor— to the Tsar himself. You've drunk yourself into a fever, you wooden-head ! "

Father Olympus stood still, turned to her, and opening wide his wrathful eyes; said impressively and harshly :

" Well ? ! "

At that the deaconess became timidly silent, walked a little way from her husband, covered her face with her handkerchief, and began to weep.

And the deacon continued his way, an immense figure, dark, majestical, like a man carved out of stone.

XIV

TEMPTING PROVIDENCE

You're always saying " accident, accident. . . ."
That's just the point. What I want to say is that on
every merest accident it is possible to look more
deeply.

Permit me to remark that I am already sixty years
old. And this is just the age when, after all the noisy
passions of his youth, a man must choose one of three
ways of life : money-making, ambition, or philosophy.
For my part I think there are only two paths.
Ambition must, sooner or later, take the form of getting
something for oneself—money or power—in acquiring
and extending either earthly or heavenly possibilities.

I don't dare to call myself a philosopher, that's too
high-flown a title for me . . . it doesn't go with my
character. I'm the sort of person who might anytime
be called upon to show his credentials. But all the
same, my life has been extremely broad and very varied.
I have seen riches and poverty and sickness, war and
the loss of friends, prison, love, ruin, faith, unbelief.
And I've even—believe it or not, as you please—
I've even seen *people*. Perhaps you think that a
foolish remark ? But it's not. For one man to see
another and understand him, he must first of all
forget his own personality, forget to consider what
impression he himself is making on his neighbours

and what a fine figure he cuts in the world. There are very few who can see other people, I assure you.

Well, here I am, a sinful man, and in my declining years I love to ponder upon life. I am old, and solitary as well, and you can't think how long the nights are to us old folk. My heart and my memory have preserved for me thousands of living recollections—of myself and of others. But it's one thing to chew the cud of recollection as a cow chews nettles, and quite another to consider things with wisdom and judgment. And that's what I call philosophy.

We've been talking of accident and fate. I quite agree with you that the happenings of life seem senseless, capricious, blind, aimless, simply foolish. But over them all—that is, over millions of happenings interwoven together, there reigns—I am perfectly certain of this—an inexorable law. Everything passes and returns again, is born again out of a little thing, out of nothing, burns and tortures itself, rejoices, reaches a height and falls, and then returns again and again, as if twining itself about the spiral curve of the flight of time. And this spiral having been accomplished, it in its turn winds back again for many years, returning and passing over its former place, and then making a new curve—a spiral of spirals. . . . And so on without end.

Of course you'll say that if this law is really in existence people would long ago have discovered it and would be able to define its course and make a kind of map of it. No, I don't think so. We are like weavers, sitting close up to an infinitely long and infinitely broad web. There are certain colours before our eyes, flowers, blues, purples, greens, all moving, moving and passing . . . but because we're so near to it we can't make out the pattern. Only those who are able to stand above life, higher than we do, gentle scholars, prophets, dreamers, saints and poets, these may have occasional glimpses through the confusion of life, and their keen inspired gaze may see the beginnings of a harmonious design, and may divine its end.

You think I express myself extravagantly? Don't you now? But wait a little; perhaps I can put it more clearly. You musn't let me bore you, though. . . . Yet what can one do on a railway journey except talk?

I agree that there are laws of Nature governing alike in their wisdom the courses of the stars and the digestion of beetles. I believe in such laws and I revere them. But there is *Something* or *Somebody* stronger than Fate, greater than the world. If it is *Something*, I should call it the law of logical absurdity, or of absurd logicality, just as you please. . . . I can't express myself very well. If it is *Somebody*, then it must be someone in comparison with whom our biblical devil and our romantic Satan are but puny jesters and harmless rogues.

Imagine to yourself an almost godlike Power over this world, having a desperate childish love of playing tricks, knowing neither good nor evil, but always mercilessly hard, sagacious, and, devil take it all, somehow strangely just. You don't understand, perhaps? Then let me illustrate my meaning by examples.

Take Napoleon : a marvellous life, an almost impossibly great personality, inexhaustible power, and look at his end—on a tiny island, suffering from disease of the bladder, complaining of the doctors, of his food, senile grumblings in solitude. . . . Of course, this pitiful end was simply a mocking laugh, a derisive smile on the face of my mysterious *Somebody*. But consider this tragic biography thoughtfully, putting aside all the explanations of learned people—they would explain it all simply in accordance with law— and I don't know how it will appear to you, but here I see clearly existing together this mixture of absurdity and logicality, and I cannot possibly explain it to myself.

Then General Skobelef. A great, a splendid figure. Desperate courage, and a kind of exaggerated belief in his own destiny. He always mocked at death, went into a murderous fire of the enemy with bravado, and courted endless risks in a kind of unappeasable thirst for danger. And see—he died on a common bed, in a hired room in the company of prostitutes. Again I say : absurd, cruel, yet somehow logical. It is as if each of these pitiful deaths by their contrast with the life, rounded off, blended, completed, two splendid beings.

The ancients knew and feared this mysterious *Someone*—you remember the ring of Polycrates— but they mistook his jest for the envy of Fate.

I assure you—*i.e.*, I don't assure *you*, but I am deeply assured of it myself—that sometime or other, perhaps after thirty thousand years, life on this earth will have become marvellously beautiful. There will be palaces, gardens, fountains. . . . The burdens now borne by mankind—slavery, private ownership of property, lies, and oppression—will cease. There will be no more sickness, disorder, death ; no more envy, no vice, no near or far, all will have become brothers. And then *He*—you notice that even in speaking I pronounce the name with a capital letter—He, passing one day through the universe, will look on us, frown evilly, smile, and then breathe upon the world—and the good old Earth will cease to be. A sad end for this beautiful planet, eh ? But just think to what a terrible bloody orgiastic end universal virtue might lead, if once people succeeded in getting thoroughly surfeited by it !

However, what's the use of taking such great examples as our earth, Napoleon, and the ancient Greeks ? I myself have, from time to time, caught a glimpse of this strange and inscrutable law in the most ordinary occurrences. If you like, I'll tell you a simple incident when I myself clearly felt the mocking breath of this god.

I was travelling by train from Tomsk to Petersburg in an ordinary first-class compartment. One of my companions on the journey was a young civil engineer, a very short, stout, good-natured young man : a simple Russian face, round, well-cared for, white eyebrows and eyelashes, sparse hair brushed up from his forehead, showing the red skin beneath . . . a kind, good " Yorkshireman." His eyes were like the dull blue eyes of a sucking pig.

He proved a very pleasant companion. I have rarely seen anyone with such engaging manners. He at once gave me his lower sleeping-place, helped me to place my trunk on the rack, and was generally so kind that he even made me feel a little awkward. When we stopped at a station he bought wine and food, and had evidently great pleasure in persuading the company to share them with him.

I saw at once that he was bubbling over with some

great inward happiness, and that he was desirous of seeing all around him as happy as he was.

And this proved to be the case. In ten minutes he had already began to open his heart to me. Certainly I noticed that directly he spoke of himself the other people in the carriage seemed to wriggle in their seats and take an exaggerated interest in observing the passing landscape. Later on, I realised that each of them had heard the story at least a dozen times before. And now my turn had come.

The engineer had come from the Far East, where he had been living for five years, and consequently he had not seen his family in Petersburg for five years. He had thought to dispatch his business in a year at the most, but at first official duties had kept him, then certain profitable enterprises had turned up, and after it had seemed impossible to leave a business which had become so very large and remunerative. Now everything had been wound up and he was returning home. Who could blame him for his talkativeness ; to have lived for five years far from a beloved home, and come back young, healthy, successful, with a heart full of unspent love ! What man could have imposed silence upon himself, or overcome that fearful itch of impatience, increasing with every hour, with every passing hundred versts ?

I soon learnt from him all about his family. His wife's name was Susannah or Sannochka, and his daughter bore the outlandish name of Yurochka. He had left her a little three-year-old girl, and " Just imagine ! " cried he, " now she must be quite grown up, almost ready to be married."

He told me his wife's maiden name, and of the poverty

they had experienced together in their early married days, when he had been a student in his last year, and had not even a second pair of trousers to wear, and what a splendid companion, nurse, mother, and sister in one, his wife had been to him then.

He struck his breast with his clenched fist, his face reddened with pride, and his eyes flashed, as he cried :

" If only you knew her ! A be-eauty ! If you're in Petersburg I must introduce you to her. You must certainly come and see us there, you must, indeed, without any ceremony or excuse, Kirochnaya 156. I'll introduce you to her, and you'll see my old woman for yourself. A Queen ! She was always the *belle* at our civil-engineers' balls. You must come and see us, I swear, or I shall be offended."

And he gave us each one of his visiting cards on which he had pencilled out his Manchurian address, and written in the Petersburg one, telling us at the same time that his sumptuous flat had been taken by his wife only a year ago—he had insisted on it when his business had reached its height.

Yes, his talk was like a waterfall. Four times a day, when we stopped at important stations, he would send home a reply-paid telegram to be delivered to him at the next big stopping-place or simply on the train, addressed to such and such a number, first-class passenger. So-and-so. . . . And you ought to have seen him when the conductor came along shouting in a sing-song tone " Telegram for first-class passenger So-and-so." I assure you there was a shining halo round his head like that of the holy saints. He tipped the conductors royally, and not the conductors only either. He had an insatiable desire to give to everybody, to make people happy, to caress them. He gave us all souvenirs, knicknacks made out of Siberian and Ural stones, trinkets, studs, pins, Chinese rings, jade images, and other trifles. Among them were many things that were very valuable, some on account of their cost, others for their rare and artistic work, yet, do you know, it was impossible to refuse them, though one felt embarrassed and awkward in receiving such valuable gifts—he begged us to accept them with such earnestness and insistence, just as one cannot continue to refuse a child who continues to ask one to take a sweet.

He had with him in his boxes and in his hand luggage a whole store of things, all gifts for Sannochka and Yurochka. Wonderful things they were—priceless Chinese dresses, ivory, gold, miniatures in sardonyx, furs, painted fans, lacquered boxes, albums—and you ought to have seen and heard the tenderness and the rapture with which he spoke of his new ones, when he showed us these gifts. His love may have been somewhat blind, too noisy, and egotistical, perhaps even a little hysterical, but I swear that through these formal and trivial veilings I could see a great and genuine love—love at a sharp and painful tension.

I remember, too, how at one of the stations when another waggon was being attached to the train, a pointsman had his foot cut off. There was great excitement, all the passengers went to look at the injured man—and people travelling by train are the most empty-headed, the wildest, the most cruel in the world. The engineer did not stay in the crowd, he went quietly up to the station-master, talked with him for a few moments, and then handed him a note for a sum of money—not a small amount, I expect, for the official cap was lifted in acknowledgment with the greatest respect. He did this very quickly ; no one but myself saw his action, but I have eyes that notice such things. And I saw also that he took advantage of the longer stoppage of the train and succeeded in sending off a telegram.

I can see him now as he walked across the platform— his white engineer's cap pushed to the back of his head ; his long blouse of fine tussore, with collar fastening at the side ; over one shoulder the strap of his field-glasses, and crossing it, over the other shoulder, the strap of his dispatch-case—coming out of the telegraph office and looking so fresh and plump and strong, with such a clear complexion, and the look of a well-fed, simple, country lad.

And at almost every big station he received a telegram. He quite spoilt the conductors—running himself to the office to inquire if there was no message for him. Poor boy ! He could not keep his joy to himself, but read his telegrams aloud to us, as if we had nothing else to think about except his family happiness—" Hope you are well. We send kisses and await your arrival impatiently.—Sannochka, Yurochka." Or : " With watch in hand we follow on the timetable the course of your train from station to station. Our spirits and thoughts are with you." All the telegrams were of this kind. There was even one like this : " Put your watch to Petersburg time, and exactly at eleven o'clock look at the star Alpha in the Great Bear. I will do the same."

There was one passenger on the train who was owner or bookkeeper, or manager of a gold mine,

a Siberian, with a face like that of Moses the Moor,[1]
dry and elongated, thick, black, stern brows, and a
long, full, greyish beard—a man who looked as if he
were exceptionally experienced in all the trials of life.
He made a warning remark to the engineer :

" You know, young man, it's no use you abusing
the telegraph service in such a way."

" What do you mean ? How is it no use ? "

" Well, it's impossible for a woman to keep herself
all the time in such an exalted and wound-up state of
mind. You ought to have mercy on other peoples'
nerves."

But the engineer only laughed and clapped the
wiseacre on the knee.

" Ah, little father, I know you, you people of the
Old Testament. You're always stealing back home
unexpectedly and on the quiet. ' Is everything as
it should be on the domestic hearth ? ' Eh ? "

But the man with the ikon face only raised his
eyebrows and smiled.

" Well, what of it ? Sometimes there's no harm in
that."

At Nizhni we had new fellow-travellers, and at
Moscow new ones again. The agitation of my engineer
was still increasing. What could be done with him ?
He made acquaintance with everybody ; talked to
married folks of the sacredness of home, reproached
bachelors for the slovenliness and disorder of bachelor
life, talked to young ladies about a single and eternal
love, conversed with mothers about their children,
and always led the conversation to talk about his

---

[1] One of the hermits of the Egyptian Desert, a saint in the
Russian Calendar,

Sannochka and Yurochka. Even now I remember that his daughter used to lisp: "I have thome yellow thlipperth," and the like. And once, when she was pulling the cat's tail, and the cat mewed, her mother said, "Don't do that, Yurochka, you're hurting the cat," and the child answered, "No, mother, it liketh it."

It was all very tender, very touching, but, I'm bound to confess, a little tiresome.

Next morning we were nearing Petersburg. It was a dull, wet, unpleasant day. There was not exactly a fog, but a kind of dirty cloudiness enveloped the rusty, thin-looking pines, and the wet hills looked like hairy warts extending on both sides of the line. I got up early and went along to the lavatory to wash; on the way I ran into the engineer, he was standing by the window and looking alternately at his watch and then out of the window.

"Good morning," said I. "What are you doing?"

"Oh, good morning," said he. "I'm just testing the speed of the train; it's going about sixty versts an hour."

"You test it by your watch?"

"Yes, it's very simple. You see, there are twenty-five sazhens between the posts—a twentieth part of a verst. Therefore, if we travel these twenty-five sazhens in four seconds, it means we are going forty-five versts an hour; if in three seconds, we're going sixty versts an hour; if in two seconds, ninety. But you can reckon the speed without a watch if you know how to count the seconds—you must count as quickly as possible, but quite distinctly, one, two, three, four, five, six—one, two, three, four, five, six—that's a *speciality* of the Austrian General Staff."

He talked on, with fidgety movements and restless eyes, and I knew quite well, of course, that all this talk about the counting of the Austrian General Staff was all beside the point, just a simple diversion of his to cheat his impatience.

It became dreadful to watch him after we had passed the station of Luban. He looked to me paler and thinner, and, in a way, older. He even stopped talking. He pretended to read a newspaper, but it was evident that it was a tiresome and distasteful occupation for him; sometimes he even held the paper upside down. He would sit still for about five minutes, then go to the window, sit down for a while and seem as if he were trying to push the train forward, then go again to the window and test the speed of the train, again turning his head, first to the right and then to the left. I know—who doesn't know?—that days and weeks of expectation are as nothing in comparison with those last half-hours, with the last quarter of an hour.

But at last the signal-box, the endless network of crossing rails, and then the long wooden platform edged with a row of porters in white aprons. . . . The engineer put on his coat, took his bag in his hand, and went along the corridor to the door of the train. I was looking out of the window to hail a porter as soon as the train stopped. I could see the engineer very well, he had got outside the door on to the step. He noticed me, nodded, and smiled, but it struck me, even at that distance, how pale he was.

A tall lady in a sort of silvery bodice and a large velvet hat and blue veil went past our carriage. A little girl in a short frock, with long, white-gaitered legs, was with her. They were both looking for someone, and anxiously scanning every window. But they passed him over. I heard the engineer cry out in a strange, choking, trembling voice :

" Sannochka ! "

I think they both turned round. And then, suddenly . . . a sharp and dreadful wail. . . . I shall never forget it. A cry of perplexity, terror, pain, lamentation, like nothing else I've ever heard.

The next second I saw the engineer's head, without a cap, somewhere between the lower part of the train and the platform. I couldn't see his face, only his bright upstanding hair and the pinky flesh beneath, but only for a moment, it flashed past me and was gone. . . .

Afterwards they questioned me as a witness. I remember how I tried to calm the wife, but what could one say in such a case ? I saw him, too—a distorted red lump of flesh. He was dead when they got him out from under the train. I heard afterwards that his leg had been severed first, and as he was trying instinctively to save himself, he fell under the train, and his whole body was crushed under the wheels.

But now I'm coming to the most dreadful point of my story. In those terrible, never-to-be-forgotten moments I had a strange consciousness which would not leave me. " It's a stupid death," I thought, " absurd, cruel, unjust," but why, from the very first moment that I heard his cry, why did it seem clear to me that the thing must happen, and that it was somehow natural and logical ? Why was it ? Can you explain it ? Was it not that I felt here the careless indifferent smile of my devil ?

His widow—I visited her afterwards, and she asked

me many questions about him—said that they both had tempted Fate by their impatient love, in their certainty of meeting, in their sureness of the morrow. Perhaps so. . . . I can't say. . . . In the East, that tried well of ancient wisdom, a man never says that he intends to do something either to-day or to-morrow without adding " *Insh-Allah*," which means, " In the name of God," or " If God will."

And yet I don't think that there was here a tempting of Fate, it seemed to me just the absurd logic of a mysterious god. Greater joy than their mutual expectation, when, in spite of distance, their souls met together—greater joy, perhaps, these two would never have experienced ! God knows what might have awaited them later ! Dischantment ? Weariness ? Boredom ? Perhaps hate ?

XV

CAIN

THE company of soldiers commanded by Captain Markof had come to take part in a punitive expedition. Tired, irritable, weary from their long journey in an uncomfortable train, the men were sullen and morose. On their arrival at a station with a strange-sounding foreign name, beer and vodka were served out to them by men who seemed to be peasants. The soldiers cried " Hurrah ! " sang songs and danced, but their faces wore a look of stony indifference.

Then the work began. The company could not be burdened with prisoners, and so all suspected persons whom they came across on the road, and all those who had no passports, were shot without delay. Captain Markof was not mistaken in his psychological analysis ; he knew that the steadily increasing irritation of his soldiers would find a certain satisfaction in such bloody chastisement.

On the evening of December 31st the company stopped for the night at a half-ruined baronial farm. They were fifteen versts from the town, and the captain reckoned to get there by three o'clock the next after-noon. He felt certain that his men would have serious and prolonged work there, and he wanted them to get whatever rest was possible, to quiet and strengthen them for it. He therefore gave orders that they be

lodged in the various barns and outhouses of the estate.
He himself occupied a large hollow-sounding, empty
room, with a Gothic fireplace, in which a bed, taken
from the local clergyman, had been placed.

A dark, starless night, windy and sleety, came
down upon the farm, swiftly and almost unnoticeably.
Alone in his immense empty chamber, Markof sat in
front of the fireplace, in which some palings from the
plundered estate were burning brightly. He put
his feet on the grate and spread out a military map
upon his bony knees, attentively studying the neighbourhood between the farm and the town. In the
red firelight his face, with its high forehead, turned-up
moustaches and firm, obstinate chin, seemed more
severe than ever.

The sergeant-major came into the room. The water
trickled down on to the floor from his waterproof
cloak. He stood still for a moment or two, and then,
convinced that the captain had not noticed his entrance,
coughed discreetly.

" Is it you ? " said the captain, bending his head
back. " What is it ? "

" Everything is in order, your honour. The third
platoon is on guard, the first division at the church
wall, the second . . ."

" All right ! What else ? Is the pass-word given ? "

" Yes, your honour. . . . " The sergeant was silent,
as if waiting to hear more, but as the captain said
nothing, he began in a lower tone,

" What's to be done, your honour, with the three
who . . ."

" Shoot them at dawn," interrupted the captain
sharply, not allowing the sergeant to finish his sentence.

" And afterwards "—he frowned and looked meaningly at the soldier—" don't ask me any more questions about them. Do you understand ? "

" Certainly, your honour," answered the soldier emphatically. . . . And they were both silent again. The captain lay down on the bed without undressing, and the sergeant remained at the door in the shadow. For some reason or other he delayed his departure.

" Is that all ? " asked the captain impatiently, without turning his head.

" Yes, that's all, your honour." The soldier fidgeted from one foot to another, and then said suddenly, with a determined resolution,

" Your honour . . . the soldiers want to know . . . what's to be done with . . . the *old* man ? "

" Get out ! " shouted the captain with sudden anger, jumping up from the bed and making as if to strike him.

The sergeant-major turned dexterously in double-quick time, and opened the door. But on the threshold he stopped for a moment and said in an official voice,

" Ah, your honour, permit me to congratulate your honour on the New Year, and to wish . . ."

" Thanks, brother," answered the captain dryly. " Don't forget to have the rifles examined more carefully to-morrow."

Left alone in the room, Markof, neither undressing nor taking off his sword, flung himself down upon the bed and lay with his face toward the fire. His countenance changed suddenly, taking on an appearance of age, and his closely-cropped head drooped on his shoulders ; his half-closed eyes wore an expression of pain and weariness. For a whole week he had suffered tortures of fever and had only overcome his illness by force of will. No one in the company knew that at nights he tossed about in fierce paroxysms, shivering in ague, delirious, only losing consciousness for moments, and then in fantastic hideous nightmares.

He lay on his back and watched the blue flames of the dying fire, feeling every moment the stealthy approaches of dizziness and weakness, the accompaniments of his usual attack of malaria. His thoughts were connected in a strange fashion with the old man who had been taken prisoner that morning, about whom the sergeant-major had just been speaking. Markof's better judgment divined that the sergeant-major had been right : there was, indeed, something extraordinary about the old man, a certain magnificent indifference to life, mingled with gentleness and a deep melancholy. People of his type, people resembling this old man, though only in a very slight degree, the captain had seen at Lao-Yan and Mukden, among the unmurmuring soldiers dying on the fields of battle. When the three men had been brought before Markof that morning, and he had explained to them by the help of cynically-eloquent gestures that they would be dealt with as spies, the faces of the two others had at once turned pale and been distorted by a deadly terror ; but the old man had only laughed with a certain strange expression of weariness, indifference, and even . . . even as it were of gentle condescending compassion towards the captain himself, the head of the punitive expedition.

" If he is really one of the rebels," Markof reflected, closing his inflamed eyes, and feeling as if a soft and bottomless abyss of darkness yawned before him, then there is no doubt that he occupies an important position among them, and I've acted very wisely in ordering him to be shot. But suppose the old man is quite innocent ? So much the worse for him. I can't spare two men to guard him, especially considering what we've got to do to-morrow. In any case, why should he escape the destiny of those fifteen whom we shot yesterday ? No, it wouldn't be fair to spare him after what we have done to others."

The captain's eyes opened slowly, and he started up suddenly in mortal terror.

Seated on a low stool by the bedside, with bent head, and the palms of his hands resting upon his knees, in a quiet and sadly thoughtful attitude, was the old man who had been sentenced to death.

Markof, though he believed in the supernatural and wore on his breast a little bag containing certain holy bones, was no coward in the general sense of the word. To retire in terror, even in the face of the most mysterious and immaterial phenomenon, the captain would have reckoned as much a disgrace as if he had fled before an enemy or uttered a humiliating appeal for mercy. With a quick, accustomed movement he drew his revolver from its leathern case and pointed it at the head of his unknown visitant, and he shouted like a madman,

" If you move, you'll go to the devil ! "

The old man slowly turned his head. Across his lips there passed that same smile which had engraved itself upon the captain's memory in the morning.

" Don't be alarmed, Captain. I have come to you without evil intention," said he. " Try to abstain from murder till the morning."

The voice of the strange visitant was as enigmatical as his smile, even monotonous, and as it were without *timbre*. Long, long ago, in his earliest childhood, Markof had occasionally heard voices like this when he had been left alone in a room, he had heard such voices behind him, voices without colour or expression, calling him by his own name. Obedient to the incomprehensible influence of this smile and this voice, the captain put his revolver under his pillow and lay down again, leaning his head on his elbow, and never taking his eyes from the dark figure of the unknown person. For some minutes the room was filled with a deep and painful silence ; there was only heard the ticking of Markof's watch, hurriedly beating out the seconds, and the burnt-out fuel in the grate falling with a weak, yet resounding and metallic, crackle.

"Tell me, Markof," began the old man at length, "what would you answer, not to a judge or to the authorities, or even to the emperor, but to your own conscience, should it ask you, ' Why did you enter upon this terrible, unjust slaughter ? ' "

Markof shrugged his shoulders as if in mockery.

"You speak rather freely, old man," said he, "for one who is going to be shot in four hours' time. However, we'll have a little conversation, if you like. It's a better occupation for me than to toss about sleeplessly in fever. How shall I answer my conscience ? I shall say first that I am a soldier, and that it is my duty to obey orders implicitly ; and secondly, I am a Russian by birth, and I would make it clear to the whole world that he who dares to rise up against the might of the great power of Russia shall be crushed as a worm under the heel, and his very tomb shall be made level with the dust. . . . "

" O Markof, Markof, what a wild and bloodthirsty pride speaks in your words ! " replied the old man. " And what untruth ! If you look at an object and put your eyes quite close to it you see only the smallest of its details, but go further away, and you see it in its true form. Do you really think that your great country is immortal ? Did not the Persians think so once, and the Macedonians, and proud Rome, who seized the whole world in her iron claws, and the wild hordes of Huns who overran Europe, and mighty Spain, lord over three-fourths of the globe ? Yet ask history what has become of their immeasurable power. And I can tell you that thousands of centuries before these there were great kingdoms, stronger, prouder, and more cultured than yours. But life, which is stronger than nations and more ancient than memorials, has swept them aside in her mysterious path, leaving neither trace nor memory of them."

" That's foolishness," objected the captain, in a feeble voice, lying down again upon his back. "History follows out its own course, and we can neither guide it nor show it the way."

The old man laughed noiselessly.

" You're like that African bird which hides its head in the sand when it is pursued by the hunter. Believe me, a hundred years hence your children's children will be ashamed of their ancestor, Alexander Vassilitch Markof, murderer and executioner."

" You speak strongly, old man ! Yes, I've heard of the ravings of those enthusiastic dreamers who want to change swords into ploughshares. . . . Ha-ha-ha !

I picture to myself the sort of state these scrofulous neurasthenists and rickety idiots of pacifists would make. No, it is only war that can forge out an athletic body and an iron character. However . . . "—Markof pressed his hand to his forehead, striving to remember something—"however, this is all unimportant. . . . But what was it I wanted to ask you ? . . . Ah, yes ! Somehow I don't think you will tell me untruths. Do you belong to these parts ? "

" No." The old man shook his head.

" But surely you were born in the district ? "

" No."

" But you are a—European ? What are you, French ? English ? Russian ? German ? "

" No, no. . . . "

Markof, in exasperation, struck the side of the bed with his fist.

" Well, who are you, then ? And why the devil do I know your face so well ? Have we ever met anywhere ? "

The old man bent his head still lower and sat for a long time saying no word. At last he began to speak, as if hesitating :

" Yes, we have met, Markof, but you have never seen me. Probably you don't remember, or you've forgotten, how once, during an epidemic of plague, your uncle hanged in one morning fifty-nine persons. I was within two paces of him that day, but he didn't see me."

" Yes . . . that's true . . . fifty-nine . . ." muttered Markof, feeling himself overwhelmed by an intolerable heat. "But they . . . were . . . rioters. . . ."

" I saw your father's cruel exploits at Sevastopol,

and your work after the capture of Ismaila," the old
man went on in his hollow voice. "Before my eyes has
been shed enough blood to drown the whole world.
I was with Napoleon on the fields of Austerlitz, Fried-
land, Jena, and Borodina. I saw the mob applauding
the executioner when he held up before them on the
platform of the guillotine the bloody head of Louis XVI.
I was present on the eve of St. Bartholomew, when the
Catholics, with prayers on their lips, murdered the
wives and children of the Huguenots. In the midst
of a crowd of enraged fanatics I gazed whilst the holy
fathers of the Inquisition burned heretics at the stake,
flayed people alive for the glory of God, and poured
white-hot lead into their mouths. I followed the hordes
of Attila, Genghis Khan, and Solyman the Magnificent,
whose paths were marked by mountains of human
skulls. I was with the noisy Roman crowd in the
circus when they sewed Christians up in the skins
of wild animals and hunted them with dogs, when they
fed the beasts with the bodies of captive slaves . . .
I have seen the wild and bloody orgies of Nero, and
heard the wailing of the Jews at the ruined walls of
Jerusalem. . . ."

" You're—only my dream . . . go away . . . you're—
only a figure in my delirium. Go away from me ! "
Markof's parched lips uttered the words with difficulty.

The old man got up from the stool. His bent
figure became in a moment immensely tall, so that
his hair seemed to touch the ceiling. He began to
speak again, slowly, monotonously, terribly :

" I saw how the blood of man was first shed upon
the earth. There were two brothers. One was
gentle, tender, industrious, compassionate ; the other,

the elder, was proud, cruel, and envious. One day they both brought offerings to the Lord according to the custom of their fathers : the younger brought of the fruits of the earth, the elder of the flesh of animals killed by him in the chase. But the elder cherished in his heart a feeling of ill-will towards his brother, and the smoke of his sacrifice spread itself out over the earth, while that of his brother ascended as an upright column to the heavens. Then the hate and envy which oppressed the soul of the elder overflowed, and there was committed the first murder on the earth . . ."

" Go away, leave me . . . for God's sake," Markof muttered to himself, and tossed about in his crumpled sheets.

" Yes, I saw his eyes grow wide with the terror of death, and his clenched fingers clutch convulsively at the sand, wet with his blood. And when after his last shudder his pale cold body lay still upon the ground, then the murderer was overwhelmed by an unbearable terror. He hid his face in his hands and ran into the depths of the forest, and lay trembling there, until at eventide he heard the voice of his offended God— ' Cain, where is thy brother Abel ? ' "

" Go away; don't torture me!" Markof's lips could scarcely move. Yet he seemed to hear the voice continue,

" In fear and trembling I answered the Lord, 'Am I my brother's keeper ? ' And then the Lord pronounced on me an eternal curse :

" ' Thou shalt remain among the number of the living as long as the earth shall endure. Thou shalt roam as a homeless wanderer through all centuries, among all nations and in all lands, and thine eyes shall behold nought but the blood shed by thee upon the earth, thine ears shall hear only the moans of the dying —eternal reminders of the brother thou hast slain.' "

There was silence for a moment, and when the old man spoke again each word fell into Markof's soul with pain:

" O Lord, how just and inexorable is Thy judgment! Already many centuries and tens of centuries have I wandered upon the earth, vainly expecting to die. A mighty and merciless power ever calls me to appear where on the battlefields the soldiers lie dead in their blood, where mothers weep, and curses are heaped upon me, the first murderer. There is no end to my sufferings, for every time I see the blood of man flowing from his body I see again my brother, stretched out upon the ground clutching handfuls of sand with his dying fingers . . . And in vain do I desire to cry out, ' Awake! Awake! Awake!' "

" Wake up, your honour, wake!" The insistent voice of the sergeant-major sounded in Markof's ears. " A telegram! . . ."

The captain was awake and on his feet in a moment. His strong will asserted itself at once, as usual. The fire had long since died out, and the pale light of dawn gleamed through the window.

" What about . . . those . . . " asked Markof, in a trembling voice.

" As you ordered, your honour, just this moment."

" But the old man ? The old man ? "

" As well."

The captain sank down upon the bed as if his strength had suddenly left him. The sergeant-major stood at attention beside him, awaiting orders.